DARK WATER

A DAN ROY THRILLER
DAN ROY SERIES, BOOK 2

Mick Bose

Join the readers group and get a free novella, Hellfire, introducing Dan Roy.
Visit http://www.mickbose.com

Also by Mick Bose:
The Dan Roy Series
Hidden Agenda (Dan Roy Series 1)
Dark Water (Dan Roy Series 2)
The Tonkin Protocol (Dan Roy Series 3)
Shanghai Tang (Dan Roy Series 4)
Scorpion Rising (Dan Roy Series 5)
Deep Deception (Dan Roy Series 6)

Enemy Within (A Standalone Thriller)

All titles available only at Amazon.

PROLOGUE

Southwest Atlanta
Georgia, USA

Vyalchek Ivanov, nickname Val, wondered if he should start torturing his captive now. The man was a whimpering mess already. He looked sick, eyes sunken, his forehead covered in sweat. A pallid crimson colored his cheeks, but otherwise the man's face was white as a sheet. He wore a suit two sizes too big on him. It had been a nice suit once, but now the elbows were threadbare, the cuffs frayed. His prominent Adam's apple bobbed over the loose collar.

Val controlled himself with an effort. The man didn't know who he was. It was better that way. He was a businessman, looking to complete a deal. Val tried to smile and spread his hands.

"Mr. Longworth, I thought we had a deal."

The man swallowed and opened his mouth, then closed it, like a fish out of water. He looked at the three men at the table next to them. Val's men. His *Bratok*. They all wore suits and had their eyes fixed on the door. Apart from the five of them, the restaurant was empty. It belonged to one of the *Bratok's* cousins. A safe place to conduct business. A waiter appeared, discreetly clearing up dishes at a table before going into the kitchen, avoiding everyone's eyes.

"Are… are these men with you?" Philip Longworth finally spoke, his voice weak. He sniffed and wiped his nose with the back of his hand.

"They are my colleagues, yes." Val regarded the man with distaste. What was he putting up his nose?

"What did you say your business was again?"

Val leaned forward slightly. Vyalchek had an imposing presence. Six four and one hundred eighty pounds, blond hair with high cheekbones and light grey eyes. Eyes that were dull, dead. Utterly devoid of feeling.

1

"Mr.. Longworth. We have been through this already. I represent a client. Our common friend has put us in contact. My client wishes to use your expertise to further his business. As proof of your abilities, he would like to know the location of the job you are currently doing." Val sat back in his chair, not wishing to intimidate the man further. There would be enough scope for that later. He held his finger up. "Make no mistake, my client is a big player in your field of work. A very big player. He would compensate you handsomely."

"How much?"

"Name your price."

Longworth looked around like he expected a grizzly bear to come out from a corner and jump on him. He caught the eyes of one of the men, who looked back at him dispassionately.

"Uh... I..."

"How about a hundred grand for starters?" Val said.

Longworth stared at him like there was a halo around his head. "A hundred grand?"

"To start with. When we check the information, if it's all there, another hundred."

Longworth was silent for a second, considering something. "How about five hundred grand, all in one go, when I get you the information?"

Val took a deep breath. *Pashli na khui,* he thought to himself. Longworth wasn't stupid. He cursed again in silence. The man looked like a junkie. Hell, he *was* a junkie—but he had brains, somehow figuring how badly Val needed this.

If this deal went down, the whole of the *Bratva* would know Val's name. Never mind the US of A. Never mind the Russkies of Brighton Beach. His name would spread to *Moskva*. To the *Krasnaya Ploshad*. Inside the Kremlin. For the first time he would have political connections. Real power. He took a sip of water and kept his face impassive.

"A hundred grand. That is all you are getting. You give us the information and you get the rest."

"If I give you the information and you vanish, who will I chase after?"

2

Longworth indicated the other three men. "Your colleagues here? I don't even know the name or identity of your client. You tell me, what security do I have that you won't just vanish with the information?"

Val narrowed his eyes. "Is that why you did not bring the drive with you today?"

Longworth nodded. "Understand my position. I'm a sole operator. If I sell you the goods, and you're not happy, you can come after me. So I don't want to sell you a dud. But if I give you the goods and wait for the money, I have no guarantee that you'll pay." He coughed and the spasm became a prolonged bout. He pulled out a handkerchief and wheezed into it. He wiped his face, mucus trailing from his lips. Val looked away in disgust. He made a pretense of checking his platinum Rolex Daytona. It was 9:30 p.m.

He asked Longworth, "Are you alright?"

"Thank you for your concern. Yes, I am."

Val lifted his chin. Was the asshole being sarcastic? He sighed. It didn't matter. "Listen to me. I can give one hundred in cash right now. In hundred dollar bills. Totally legit money. We can pick you up tomorrow, like we did today. You must have the hard drive tomorrow. When we have it, we check it on a laptop here." Val was stabbing his finger on the table. "If it's all good, then you have the remaining money."

"I want four hundred."

"What?"

Longworth made a sound like he was choking. He cleared his throat and swallowed noisily. Val grimaced.

"Four hundred tomorrow on delivery. Otherwise, I don't want your money."

"If I say no?"

"Then the deal is off." Longworth put his hat on and got up slowly. Val didn't move a muscle. He glanced sideways at one of his *Bratok*, who stood up to get in Longworth's face. The man had a barrel chest, and his jacket moved to reveal the gun inside a shoulder holster. Longworth stopped, alarmed.

"Who *are* you guys?"

"You can ask your friend. I just want to know if we have a deal or not?"

"For four hundred on delivery, yes we do."

Val shut his eyes a moment. A few choice Russian phrases came to his mind. "Okay. Four hundred, if we can check it here on delivery tomorrow. There will be a map, yes?"

Longworth nodded. "Yes, there will be. I want the hundred now."

Val reached inside his jacket. Longworth's eyes bulged in fear for a second, then calmed when he saw the key. Val who motioned to one of his men and gave him the key. The man reached a hand underneath the table and pulled out a briefcase. He unlocked it, snapped it open and put the briefcase in front of Longworth.

Val eyed Longworth closely. "It's all in there. You can count it if you want."

Longworth raised his eyes to Val. "I'm sure it's all there." Val did not change his expression.

Longworth coughed. "Do you mind if I use the bathroom?"

Val gestured to another of his *Bratok*, as broad as the last one. "He will show you."

"Thanks."

They walked to the rear of the restaurant. The place was small, about thirty tables laid out in a square formation. A sign outside said, "St Petersburg, Authentic Russian Cuisine". The interior was simple, red and blue curtains hanging above windows with neon lights. A selection of Russian dolls adorned the main counter. Longworth and the man moved through a beaded curtain at the back. Val sat, tapping the desk with his fingers.

There was a crashing sound, then a shout from the rear. A car engine roared, tires screeching. More shouts. Val was up and out the front door before any of his men, his 0.357 Smith and Wesson in his hand. He ran around the corner just in time to see a blue car, belching smoke, take a right at the end of the road. The *Bratok* supposed to guard Longworth came running, pointing at a window.

"He opened the bathroom window and jumped. Jesus Christ. The car was waiting for him. He planned the whole thing!"

Val turned on him, his face a mask of hatred. His fist lashed out, making solid connection with the man's chin. The *Bratok* stumbled backwards. Val punched him in the head again and the man went down. Snarling with fury, Val began kicking until the face was a mess of blood and bone.

Then he aimed his gun at the unmoving body and squeezed the trigger twice. The man's body jerked as the rounds slammed into it. Val swung the gun towards the other men, who stepped back.

"Find him!" Val screamed. "Or all of you are dead!"

CHAPTER 1

North Bethesda, Virginia
Present day

Dan Roy stood with his head bowed.

The little cemetery faced the church. It was August, and high above, white clouds sailed in a silent blue sky. The church was pretty, with a spire rising above the green trees hanging around it. Around him, Dan could hear the chirping of birds. Up here, there was no sound of traffic. He was alone in the cemetery.

Every year, he made this journey. For him, it was a pilgrimage. He kneeled, and put the two bouquets of flowers by the two gravestones that stood side by side. Rita and Duncan Roy. His parents. They had given him the best life they could. It seemed like a long time ago.

The sadness he got used to, but the sense of loss was ever present. A chasm that would never be filled. He arranged the flowers around, and touched the gravestones.

Dan whispered, "Words will never express how much I miss you."

He touched his hands on the gravestones and kept them there for a while. It felt cold. He swallowed hard, and felt the sting behind his eyes. He got up, turned around and left.

It was the only emotion he allowed himself. Years in the Delta Force, and then in black ops for Intercept, had made him an automaton. A fighting machine. The best that Intercept, one of the most powerful black ops outfits, had in their possession.

But a machine nevertheless. Deployed globally, working solo, and at short notice. There was never time for himself, or his own thoughts. He came here once every year, in rain, snow and sunshine. Somehow, it allowed him to heal, and to feel a sense of peace.

Some things in life lasted for ever.

*****

Dan got into his car and roared down the highway. His hands gripped the steering wheel lightly. As he drove, his dark eyes glanced at the rear-view, checking out the cars driving behind him.

As the Virginia countryside flashed by, he wondered what direction his life would take in the future. He was in the process of selling his parents' house in Bethesda. Once that was done, the last physical bond he had would disappear. He was free to go where he wanted.

It was not merely new vistas that he wanted to see. He wanted to open new doors in his mind, too. Look at the world with new eyes. Constant violence had wrapped a wintry cloak around his soul.

He *was* a man of violence, he could not deny that. But he was also a human being. One with sorrow, regrets, happiness like everyone else. For too long, he had been forced to operate like a machine. A part of him liked that. It was who he was. But another part of him wanted…wanted some warmth. Some life.

That process had started in London, two months ago. But it had not lasted long. He had been framed for a crime he did not commit, and the true perpetrator had killed his old commanding officer. Like a crazed bull, Dan had fought back.

That had been the final break. Intercept had agreed to let him go. He needed to have one last meeting with the man who had become his new handler. A man called McBride, but he suspected that might not be his real name. It did not matter. McBride possessed real power in the corridors of the Pentagon, and in Capitol Hill. Like most of the Intercept handlers did.

Dan drove down south from Arlington. Straight down the I-95, and to a town adjacent to Fort Belvoir. He drove past the Davison Airfield, a military airport he had taken flights from in the past. He felt a familiar tightness in his stomach. That pre-mission coiling of the limbs. The smell of impending combat.

He would miss it. It was what he did. He was a warrior, and always would be. Dan parked the car on the street where he was due to meet McBride. After five minutes of waiting, he saw two black Ford SUV's park at the end of the street. Dan watched them park, and turn their engines off.

He got out and stretched his six feet, two-hundred-and-twenty-pound frame. The width of his shoulders and chest accounted for most of that. He locked his car, then approached the second of the two SUV's. The door slid open. Inside, he saw an older man, in his late fifties. His salt and pepper hair was brushed back neatly. He was dressed in a black suit, which seemed to be the unofficial uniform for Intercept employees. Only, McBride was much more than an employee. It was rumoured he was high up in the Pentagon. Dan would never know his real identity, and he did not care.

More than anything, Dan wanted to be free.

"Close the door, Dan," McBride said.

Dan sat down next to him. The older man said, "Sorry to hear you are leaving. Any particular reason?"

Dan said, "Nothing particular."

"I am sorry about Guptill, too. I know he was your CO."

Dan did not say anything. John Guptill had been Dan's handler in Intercept, and his mentor when he had joined Squadron B, SFOD-D, as the Delta Forces were known. Last year, Guptill had been killed. Dan had found the killer.

Dan did not mind risking his life. Hell, he lived for it. But he wasn't so crazy about the games intelligence agencies and politicians played. Those games wrecked innocent lives.

McBride leaned forward. His slate grey eyes were steely. "You know this is your exit interview, right?"

Dan nodded. Every Intercept agent had one. They were held to a code of silence so strict, any break of it resulted in certain death. Not just death. A disappearance. The bodies were never found.

For the next half hour, Dan answered questions about his motives and future plans. At the end, McBride leaned back. He opened the window. He clipped the end of a cigar and lit it up. There was a sign in the car that said no smoking, but not many people told McBride what he could or could not do.

Dan liked that about him.

Between puffs of fragrant tobacco, McBride said, "Head out to the south. Georgia or Florida. Catch some rays."

Dan said, "I'll think about it."

"Hey, as part of your bonus, we'll get you a one-way flight."

They had talked about money already. A healthy seven figure sum. The price paid for conducting the most dangerous, and deniable missions in hotspots around the world.

And the price of silence.

Dan made for the door. "Like I said, I'll think about it."

CHAPTER 2

Val Ivanov looked out the tinted windows of his Cadillac as the car smoothly pulled up outside the warehouse in Marietta. The largest city of Cobb County, northwest of Atlanta, and prime Mexican gang land. A gang called Z9, or Zapato 9 as they were better known, had called for this meeting. Val hadn't agreed initially until he heard their request. It was of mutual benefit. Besides, alliances between the *Bratva* and the large Mexican gangs weren't uncommon. In California, Nevada, Texas, all the way down to Florida, wise guys had to work with Mexican gangs. They ruled the turf. They were well-organized and by sheer numbers they threatened everybody. Working with them opened up multiple revenue pathways. Something the Cosa Nostra hadn't learnt yet. Alliances between the Sicilians and Mexicans were rare. Well, Val thought, their mistake was his opportunity.

Val glanced at the *Bratok* next to him. Artin was his personal bodyguard. He was lightning quick with a Glock, and equally skilled with an AK-74. He had saved Val's life more than once.

"How many men at the back?" Val asked.

"Three. And three opposite the front and sides. We have the place surrounded. Anything happens to us, no one leaves alive."

Another Cadillac stopped in front and four of his men were out, stretching. None wore suits today, including Val. He was pleased with the precautions they had taken, but he knew the Mexicans wouldn't try anything. They didn't want to start a war. It interrupted business and helped no one.

The front door of the warehouse opened and a Hispanic kid stepped out. His forearms were covered in tattoos. Indigo, maroon and blue, with Latin inscriptions. A gun was stuck in plain view in his belt. He waved at them. Val waited until Artin got out the other side, came to his door and opened it. It was good to make an entrance. He was a *Pakhan*, after all. A general, a godfather. Eight cells under his control in Atlanta and Jacksonville. Damn right he was going to make an entrance.

Val stepped out eventually, dwarfing the other men around him. They knew the drill. Two stood to either side of him, one in front, the rest at the back. In that formation, they approached the lone gang member. Val had to duck inside the door as one of his men held it open.

It was darker inside, but light streamed in through the windows on the roof. Val guessed the gang used this warehouse as a meeting point. It was clean and well-maintained. A stairway went around the sides, circling the perimeter. He spotted two men with rifles. In the middle of the floor, a table had been laid out with simple wooden chairs. Four men sat around it. All of them looked older than the kid who greeted them. From their late twenties to early forties, he guessed. The man in the middle wore a red bandana and he seemed the oldest. At the back, there was an open door with another gang member standing guard.

Val approached the four men, who stood up. The man with the red bandana was the first to shake his hand.

"Manolo," Val said. Manolo Estefan. A mid-ranking captain who was making moves for the top. Val pointed at the armed men above.

"You expecting trouble?"

"Only if it's coming our way," Manolo said, his hard, glittering black eyes not leaving Val's face. The men on either side of him started to look around. Val's men had formed a loose semi-circle around him.

Val shrugged. "Putting snipers around us is not a great way to start a meeting."

"Do you expect me to believe you have not surrounded the place with your own men?"

They stared at each other in silence. Above them, there was a soft clicking sound. Safety catches on rifles being released. It all happened very quickly. In a blur of movement, men had their guns out. There was a shout from the back, and the snipers leaned over the rails with their rifles trained.

Val shook his head, his face blank. "You start this, Manolo, we go all the way. It never stops. I promise you."

Manolo smiled. "This is our territory. If all of us spit on you, you will drown."

"Won't matter to you, if you're dead. You know who I am. I don't make empty threats."

"My boys are angry. The gringo robbed them."

"Then let's talk business."

Manolo stared at him for another second, then signaled to his men. The guns were lowered slowly.

"Stand down," Val told Artin. He sat down, while his men stood behind him. The four Mexicans sat down facing him.

"Tell me what the gringo has done to you."

"Half a kilo of cocaine has gone. The gringo was selling for us. He never paid us. He was going to turn up with the money. He never did."

Val breathed out. Philip Longworth had guts. Taking on the Z9. And now the *Bratva*. Well, he was going to pay for it.

"What has he done to you?" Manolo asked. Val told him.

Manolo said, "What do we do now?"

Val shifted in his chair. Damn thing was uncomfortable. "We start with his house. Ransack the place. Top to bottom. Your half kilo might well be there hidden."

And maybe what we need as well, he thought to himself.

Manolo nodded. "Let's do it."

CHAPTER 3

The woman in front of Dan stumbled over her suitcase. Dan leaned forward and picked it up for her. She had been in the seat next to him in the flight from Washington Dulles to Atlanta. Her dark hair was tied back in a ponytail. Her skin was tanned from the sun, and she had brown eyes. In her fifties, he guessed. She had bags under her eyes, and looked tired.

Hartsfield-Jackson airport was busy. The air conditioning was keeping the place cool, but Dan knew it was hot outside. High eighties, he reckoned from the sun that beamed in through the windows. They had just taken their luggage off the conveyor belt when the woman had slipped. Dan had his usual single backpack. All his belongings in one place.

The woman said, "Thank you."

"No problem," Dan said. The woman flashed him a tired smile, then went on her way towards the exit. Dan followed at a more leisurely pace. Although the airport pulsed with activity, Dan was relaxed. It was his first vacation in years. Intercept worked very much like Delta Forces – when not deployed he had to undertake constant training and mock battles. This time, he would go where he wanted to, and just drift as far down south as he could. All the way to the Florida Keys, and then to the Caribbean. He was looking forward to it.

He came outside, and felt the heat hit him immediately. The sun was blinding. He wiped sweat off his forehead, feeling like he needed a sweatband. Must be in the mid-nineties at least, he thought. His cream T-shirt—he had deliberately chosen a light color—was sticking to his back like a second skin. He passed a billboard where the date, time and weather were displayed. Ninety-four degrees. Seventy-two percent humidity.

He walked to the queue for cabs. While he was waiting, he looked opposite, where car drivers were picking up their loved ones. Hugs and hellos. Something Dan had never experienced. Apart from his parents he had no family. He had always travelled alone.

As he watched, he noticed the same woman standing at the far corner. Near the edge of the sidewalk with her suitcase, like she was waiting for someone. She looked in Dan's direction, and their eyes met. For a moment, Dan recognized a vulnerability in her eyes. Then she looked away quickly, like she was afraid of something.

He saw the snout of a tan Chevrolet sedan appear around the corner. The car stopped in front of the woman. She did not move. Dan saw a tall blonde man step out. He was dressed in a suit. His movements were slow and deliberate. Two other men stepped out from the back. Also in suits. Shorter, but wider, with bulges of shoulder holsters at their armpits. Their eyes darted around, looking at cars, people.

Dan knew bodyguards when he saw them. The tall blond man towered over the woman, who seemed to shrink away from him. He spoke to her, and Dan could see her shaking her head. The tall man said something again, which drew the same response. One of the bodyguards was standing behind the woman. The driver was in the car, engine running, and the kerbside back door was open.

It happened in a flash. That corner of the sidewalk was empty. No one noticed.

The bodyguard clamped a meaty hand over the woman's face. He almost lifted her up, and propelled her inside the back seat. Before she disappeared inside the car, she raised her head. She looked up and met Dan's eyes once more. For the briefest of seconds. But enough to communicate a vital message.

Help me.

The trunk was opened and the woman's suitcase was chucked inside. With a slam of doors and a screech of tires, the sedan took off towards the exit.

Dan had a split second to decide his next course of action. He had the choice of not doing anything. But if he did, then, potentially, the vortex of death and violence would open for him again.

Dan was almost at the head of the queue. There was a guy ahead of him. A single man. Dan acted quickly. As the cab drew up, Dan pushed the man to one side.

"Hey", the man shouted, as he stumbled to the side.

Dan said, "I'm sorry, but there's an emergency."

The man had fallen over, and he was scrambling to his feet as Dan got inside the cab and slammed the door shut.

"Drive, now," he said to the driver. The cab pulled out, and the man Dan had pushed to one side stood up, shouting and shaking his fist.

The driver looked at Dan in the rear view. "Lookin' for someone, mister?"

"Yes. A tan sedan. Chevrolet. Took the downtown exit."

"I'm on it," said the driver. Dan kept a look out the window. Several cars had slowed down ahead, looking for the right turn to take. Dan's driver zipped around them expertly. Soon he pointed up ahead.

"Tan sedan, three cars up on left lane."

Dan followed his gaze and saw the car. The same one with the woman in it. He could see the shape of the two bodyguards on either side with someone in between.

"Stay on this lane and follow them," Dan said.

"No sweat," said the driver. "You an undercover cop?"

"If I was I couldn't tell you, could I?"

The man smiled in the rear-view mirror. "Cool."

Traffic flowed steadily, a metallic river on the highway. They passed industrial estates, then lush grasslands on either side. They probably belonged to the colleges, Dan thought. Farther north, in the distance he could see the shining towers of downtown winking in the sunlight. They passed Georgia State University. Traffic began to get heavier as they approached downtown.

The sedan took a turn soon. Dan's driver waited and then followed. This part of downtown did not seem so salubrious. Derelict buildings stood on either side. Shopping trolleys and trash cans littered the small green parks. They drove through till they came to an intersection. They stopped at a warehouse, and the gates opened. The sedan drove in. Dan's cab had stopped at the mouth of the street. Dan waited for ten seconds after the gates shut. He paid the driver with a fifty-dollar bill and got out.

"Keep the change," Dan said, when the driver wound the window down.

"You be careful, pal," the driver said. He drove off. Dan hitched both straps of the backpack on his back. He stood for a while against a disused shop awning. The walls surrounding the warehouse were more than six feet tall. Inside he could see the steel roof of the main building. The warehouse was used, but it had no signs in front. There was a path going around the back.

Dan headed for the path. He took a trash can and turned it upside down, emptying it. Then he used it to stand up on the back wall of the warehouse. No barbed wire. There was a row of short spikes, but he could climb over that easily. He looked over. Six feet fall, roughly. A cluster of refuse sacks below. He would fall on them, that would mask the sound. Was there an alarm? If there was, it might be off in daytime. He would have to take that chance. Against the main warehouse building, he could see the parked sedan. It was empty.

Dan lifted himself up, and pushed himself on the wall. He vaulted over the spikes, sailing through air. His aim was to land on his feet, but roll over quickly so his feet did not take the whole impact. He landed on the black refuse sacks. He slid down and was on his feet quickly. Two smaller outbuildings flanked the main warehouse. He noticed the cameras on either side of the warehouse, facing front and back. He was being watched. Not much he could do about that.

Dan flitted across the courtyard like a shadow. He was against the door of the warehouse. It was a glass double door, and it did not seem locked. He crouched against the side wall. No one came in or out. Staying crouched, Dan pushed the glass door and went inside. There was a lobby, with a desk, but it was dark. A door at the end which led to main atrium of the warehouse. Dan took the backpack off, and crawled forward on his hands and knees.

He came against the door and lifted his head up to peek in the glass panel. Suddenly, something was jammed against his back. The muzzle of a gun.

"Stay quiet," a voice said. "Get your hands in the air."

CHAPTER 4

Dan stood very still. He had been listening out for movement, but this guy had been very quiet. He was good.

The voice said with more menace, "Get your fucking hands up. Or I shoot."

Slowly Dan lifted his hands up. He felt himself being patted down. Dan listened hard and he turned his head sideways. He could not see anyone. The lights were off but there was sunlight coming from outside, enough to afford visibility. The man was on his own. While he was searching Dan, he had moved his gun from Dan's back. He was bending down on his knees, searching Dan's legs for a concealed weapon.

His own weapon was in the air. Dan had a second, maybe two. It was all the time Dan needed. He kicked out backwards, the heel of his trunk catching the man's gun arm. The movement was totally unexpected. The man grunted as his arm was thrown back. In the same movement, Dan turned sideways and fell on top of the man.

He saw Dan coming, and raised the gun. But Dan was quicker, and he had gravity on his side. Their bodies collided, and Dan reached for the gun arm. His fingers curled around the man's wrist, and smashed it against the floor. Dan felt a sharp punch land against his right ribs. The blow was vicious, but Dan ignored it. He lifted up the gun wrist and smashed it down on the carpeted floor again. The gun flew out of the man's hand.

Before the man could hit him again, Dan had drawn his right arm back. He crashed it down with a straight punch aimed at the jaw. The man's head snapped sideways. He reached his arm up and tried to hook his fingers into Dan's eyes. Dan felt the nails scrape his cheek. He lifted himself up and straddled the man on his chest. Two quick blows, using both fists, rocked the man's head from side to side like a rag doll. Dan felt bone crunch against the jaws, and the body became still.

Dan came off him, and picked up the gun. A Colt M191. He checked the rounds. Six left. He slid back the safety and approached the door again. Three of the bodyguards were inside. He couldn't see the tall blond guy. The woman was in the middle of the room, tied to a chair. One of the men was talking to her. The other two stood to the side, facing the woman. Dan craned his neck up. A steel cage walkway went around the perimeter. It was empty. There was no one else inside.

Dan looked behind. This guy would wake up soon. Then it would be four against one, minimum. He had to act now. He pushed open the door a fraction. He went to the floor and slowly crawled out.

The woman saw him first. The man talking to her followed her gaze. With a shout, he reached for his shoulder holster. He did not get the chance to draw it. Dan fired, double tapping the man on the face. His head exploded into a geyser of blood and bone, and some of the tissue fell on the woman. She screamed.

Four rounds left. No margin for error.

The other two men had turned. One of them was half pointing his gun at Dan, when the slug tore into him. It hit him on the neck, and he went down. The gun fired, the round going high in the air. Dan could not kill him now, while the other guy had enough time to take his weapon out and aim.

The sound of the unsuppressed weapons was like small explosions. Another loud bang, and a piece of wood inches from Dan's face flew off the door. Dan rolled over, knowing the man would have to re aim for him. He came up shooting. His aim was off as a result but he caught the man in the shoulder with the first round, spinning him backwards. He screamed, and tried to fire again, and this time Dan shot him between the eyes. He toppled back and fell with a crash. Dan had turned his weapon already to the remaining guy. He was still twitching. His arm still held the weapon.

All of six seconds had elapsed since Dan fired the first shot.

Dan walked over calmly. He ignored the woman, who was staring at him with bulging eyes. He kicked the gun away from the man's hand. The bullet had gone through the side of the neck and come out the other side. It had severed the man's cervical spinal cord in the neck. He was trying to move, but all he could do was twitch. Dan bent down over him.

"Who do you work for?" he asked.

The man's eyes were glazed. They looked at Dan without seeing. Dan had seen the look before. Brainstem death. The man could not speak if he tried. Death would come soon as the lungs stopped inflating.

Dan walked over to the door to check on the guy outside. The man was still out cold. Dan slapped him on the cheek. Hard, twice. Still out cold. He fished around in his pockets. He found a six-inch K bar knife in the front belt. He took it, and walked back to the woman. He cut through her ropes quickly. The woman finally found her voice.

"Who are you?" she gasped. Dan was leaning over the guy, frisking him. He stood up, having found nothing.

"We need to get out of here, quickly." Dan ran over to the remaining body and searched. Apart from another Colt he found nothing. He stretched out his hand towards the older woman. She took it willingly. They crossed over the guy who was out cold on the reception floor.

The sedan was open. "Get in," Dan said. The keys were in the ignition. He fired the engine. He took the two Colts out, and put one between his legs on the car seat. He checked the other one – five rounds left. He gave it to the woman.

He asked, "You fired a gun before?"

"No."

"Just hold the butt, don't touch the trigger. Get your head below the window. Give me the gun when I ask for it."

In silence, the woman nodded. Dan turned the sedan and approached the gate. As he had expected, the steel gates slid open into a recess in the walls. Dan drove out fast.

CHAPTER 5

"Where do you live?" Dan asked the woman. They were in downtown traffic now, and she was sitting up straighter. Dan kept a look out in all directions as he drove. He did not get an answer from her.

He said, "Hey. Are you ok?"

The woman was staring ahead, and she turned at his voice. Dan saw the fear in her eyes. She swallowed and said, "Yes, uh, I'm fine."

"What's your name?"

"Jody. Jody Longworth."

"Jody, where do you live?"

She pressed her hands against her forehead. "Up from downtown. Towards Virginia Highlands. Just head north."

Dan checked the signs. He was headed in the right direction. He gave Jody a few minutes. Traffic was light in the midmorning hour.

Then he said, "My name is Dan Roy."

The woman sniffed into a piece of tissue, and nodded. "Hi, Dan."

"Why were those men after you?"

Jody did not reply for several seconds. Then she said, "It's a long story. I…" She looked at Dan. "I don't even know who you are."

Just someone who has a habit of getting into trouble, Dan thought to himself.

Out loud, he said, "Just here on vacation."

"Vacation, huh?"

"Yeah."

"Where did you learn to shoot like that?"

Dan said, "I used to be in the army."

Jody was silent. Dan was wondering if they should head to the nearest police station. He never had much luck with police. They would not believe him, and probably arrest him. He never carried any creds. With Intercept, he was not *allowed* any creds. Still, the police would give the woman some safety.

He said, "Maybe we should go to the cops."

The look of fear returned on the woman's eyes. "No," she shook her head.

"You scared of those guys?"

Jody was silent again. Dan sneaked a glance at her. Her face was lowered and her hands were knotted on her lap. He tried a different approach.

He asked, "Have you ever seen these guys before?"

Jody pointed with her hand. "It's this turning up here," she said.

Dan indicated and said, "You didn't answer my question."

"Like I said, long story."

"Must be, for them to grab you the way they did."

Jody did not answer. Dan drove up a narrow, secluded road, following the signs for Virginia Highlands.

"This is me," Jody said, and Dan pulled to a stop outside a house set way back from the road. Jody opened the passenger door and got out. She shut it gently and looked at Dan.

She said, "Listen Dan, I really appreciate what you did back there. I don't know how to thank you. Would you like to come in for a cup of coffee?"

Dan drummed his fingers on the steering wheel, and looked out the window at Jody's house.

The front lawn was overgrown. The letterbox was bare. Jody must have emptied it recently. The house was modern, what realtors liked calling the Bauhaus style. It had a wooden front that matched the surrounding tall trees. A balcony with a glass railing ran around the top floor. The curtains were open, the garage door shut. Pine trees creaked high above. It smelled of musk, earth and acorns. It was very quiet. Similar houses on either side. Some bigger, some smaller.

The street was deserted. Dan watched the pine trees move in the breeze. Funny, seeing pine trees in Atlanta. Planted in this suburban neighborhood for effect. The thick branches brushed against the distant blue sky, pulling white clouds in their wake.

Dan said, "I don't want to impose on you. You have family in there?"

A shadow passed over Jody's face. "Not now, no. My husband is away with work."

Dan said, "Well, guess I'll leave you to it, then."

Jody turned to him. "No, honestly, it's no problem. You must want some coffee, right?"

Dan nodded. "I could use a cup of coffee."

Jody gave him a tired smile. "Of course. Come on in."

Dan stepped out and locked the car. Jody was standing close by, looking around her, like she was expecting to see someone. Not normal behavior for someone who'd just got home, Dan thought. He walked around the front of the car.

Dan said, "You ok, Jody?"

She had that look on her face again. The frightened, hunted look.

"Yes, fine. Come on." She started to walk up the brick path in the front garden. She looked left and right. Dan walked behind her, watching her movements. Jody went up to the front door and paused. A heavy, brown oakwood front door. Jody hesitated for a few seconds, then dug into her pocket, searching for a key.

While she was doing that, Dan stepped to the side and peered in through the living room window. He stopped short.

"Jody," he called out. She flinched at her name being called.

Dan said, "Don't open the door."

CHAPTER 6

Jody tiptoed over, and joined Dan by the window. The room was clearly visible through a gap in the curtains. Without saying anything, Dan pointed.

The room was large, thirty by twenty feet. L-shaped comfortable sofas were arranged around a flat screen TV. The TV was face-down on the carpet. The sofas had their cushions removed and it looked like someone had taken a knife and sliced round the edges. Foam spilled out on the threadbare carpet. Framed photos from the wall had been taken down and smashed on the floor.

Dan could feel Jody shivering next to him. Her hand was at her throat. "Oh, my God," she said in a trembling voice. Gently, Dan put an arm on her shoulder. He fished in his pocket and took out the car keys.

He spoke in a low voice. "Go and sit down in the car Jody. I wanna take a look around."

Jody did not seem to hear him. She was looking at the scene inside, transfixed.

"Oh my God," she repeated. Dan had not lived in a home for most of his adult life. He wondered what it was like coming home to see it trashed like this. He took her elbow and guided her back to the car. Jody was breathing hard, and she walked down the brick path bisecting the overgrown front lawn without saying a word.

Dan left her in the car, took the house keys from her, and walked back up to the front door.

He checked the window and door frames. No sign of forced entry.

To the left of the front garden, there was a path that went around to the rear. Dan walked around the house, standing on his tiptoes to peer into the kitchen window. The kitchen had cabinet doors on the walls above the sink and on the sides, all open, plates smashed on the floor. Dan picked up his pace.

At the rear of the house, bi-folding doors opened up the kitchen and dining area into the patio. He stood on the patio and looked out at the garden. It was smaller than he had imagined. Maybe the front lawn took up too much of the land. The pine trees continued in the back, screening the end of the garden. On both sides, houses stood on similar plots of land.

He went back around to the front door, unlocked it and gently pushed it open, listening intently. No sound, apart from the pine trees swaying in the breeze. If there was someone still in there, they were being mighty quiet.

He stepped in. The alarm didn't go off as he had expected. It only reinforced his heightened state of awareness. His hand went to his beltline automatically, feeling for the Glock.

Silence around him still. He crept down the hallway. He didn't go into the living room. Straight ahead, he saw the staircase, and the entrance to the kitchen. He bent his knees, lowering himself to offer a smaller target if someone emerged from the kitchen. On his tiptoes, he went forward. The floorboards had seen better days. A couple creaked and Dan grimaced.

He stayed low and entered the kitchen. It was a large space. The table hadn't been touched, but the cushions of the chairs had been knifed. The walls had some modern art, framed and tasteful. He had no idea about modern art, but these looked nice. All the drawers had been opened. He found a kitchen knife and stuck it in his back belt.

Next, Dan crept up the stairs. It felt like clearing a house in Iraq or Afghanistan. Only this time he didn't have his trusted Heckler and Koch 416 rifle. He tested each stair before he put his full weight on them. At the top of the stairs was the master bedroom with the balcony in the front. The back bedroom probably had one as well. To his right a small corridor. He craned his neck. It led to a bathroom and another bedroom. The silence was pin-drop now, the sound of the pine trees left outside.

To be safe, he dropped and crawled into the master bedroom. The bedding was on the floor and the bed frame had been taken apart. The wardrobe doors were open, clothes spilled on the floor. He checked the other bedrooms quickly. All had been systemically turned out and searched. Paintings and framed photos had been taken off walls. Floorboards had been lifted up. Air conditioners in every room had been loosened from their wall sockets.

This was a professional job. Not some ordinary burglar.

He went to the room next to the bathroom. It was a study, the walls lined with shelves. Books had been tipped off the shelf and lay in a disorderly pile on the floor. He picked one up. It was a bound version of a technical journal, *Optical Fibers*. He waded through the strewn books and magazines on the floor. He picked up one glossy magazine and flipped through it. It was called *Communications*. A page inside had been folded on an article called, *Network processing in high pressure marine environment*. Whatever the hell that meant.

He looked at the authors' names in the credits. Philip Longworth was the top one. Must be Jody's husband. It seemed as if Philip was a cable engineer. He must have been an important one to write articles.

At the desk he saw the wires for the broadband modem. There was a window above the desk that faced the road outside. He peered underneath. Telephone wires sticking out, and a panel of electric sockets. He checked the drawers of the table. All empty. There was a filing cabinet with its doors open. He couldn't see a laptop.

Dan got up and walked around the second floor. He went out on the back-bedroom balcony and looked at the garden. Then he went downstairs, and walked out to the car.

Jody was sitting inside, biting her nails. She looked up as Dan approached. Dan walked over to the driver's seat and shut the door.

He said, "We need to call the cops."

Jody's voice was strained. "What's happened in there? I need to see."

Dan said, "Someone has taken the place apart, Jody. You wanna tell me what they were looking for?"

Her face was ashen. "I...I don't know," she said.

Dan sighed. "Ok, Jody, we can do this two ways. Either you tell me, and then we think about what to do next, or I drive to the nearest cop precinct and leave you there to tell them."

Jody had her hands folded on her lap, and her neck was bowed.

Dan spoke softly. "It's those same guys, right? Are they after your husband? He owes them money?"

Jody's head shot up. She looked at Dan with wide eyes. "What do you know about my husband?"

"Nothing," Dan said. "I think his study upstairs has been trashed. I saw a magazine with his name on it. Philp Longworth, right?"

"Yes."

"I'm just guessing here, Jody. When this kind of stuff happens, it's either for money or something valuable."

Jody was silent. She looked at house, then at the road, then back at the house again. Like she was trying to gather up the courage to go inside, but not sure she wanted to.

Dan said, "Who were those guys at the airport, Jody?"

"I have never seen them before."

"You sure?"

She nodded, her eye downcast again. "Never seen them, but…"

"But?"

"Seen some other guys…two of them. They used to park here, outside, opposite the house." Jody pointed with a finger.

"What sort of a car did they drive?"

"A blue Chrysler."

Jody wiped her eyes and sniffed.

"Philip's been very busy with work lately. Gets up early, comes home late. He said he had something important to do in Barnham, near the coast, and headed out there. That's the last I heard of him."

"Where's Barnham?" Dan asked.

"It's a small town not far from St Mary's." Dan knew of the little historic town, near the ocean in Georgia.

"Was something bothering him?" Dan asked.

"He never said anything."

Dan said, "These two men waiting in the Chrysler, what did they look like?"

"Hispanic, I think. Can't be sure. But I saw them all the time, sitting in their car on the curb opposite. Watching me."

"Did you tell the cops?"

Jody nodded. "Yes."

"What have they said?"

"They asked me questions, then went around to his employer as well."

"And?"

"Nothing. His employer has given the police details of where he was living in Barnham. The place is empty and there is no sign of Philip."

Dan said, "So Philip's not come back?"

"No. There's no sign of him. No one knows where he is."

"Have you spoken to the cops again to see if anything's changed?"

Jody pursed her lips. Dan said, "Jody, the sooner we get to the bottom of this the better. We've come this far, don't hold out on me now."

Jody's face was ashen. "You don't understand." Her voice trembled. She sniffed and Dan turned to look at her. Jody's face was chalk white. Her nose became red and tears welled in her eyes.

Dan fished around in his pockets and came out with a handkerchief. He gave it to her. She accepted it without a word.

Jody said, "You can't help me. And I can't go back to the cops. The cops only came around because someone from his office informed them. I didn't."

Dan lowered his voice. "Why not?"

"Because they'll kill my little girl."

CHAPTER 7

Dan rested his head back on the seat. It made sense now. The old woman had no family apart from her daughter and husband, and these scumbags had threatened her daughter's life to keep her quiet. Dan waited, giving Jody space.

After a while, she spoke again. "I was going out grocery shopping one day. The men in the blue Chrysler drove after me. I stopped by at a drugstore on the way. It was quiet in the parking lot and they came up to me. They had tattoos all over them. One of them wanted to see my husband. I told them, he was gone with work. At first, I denied knowing where he was. But then I had to tell them the truth."

Dan said, "When they mentioned your daughter?"

"Yes. I don't know how they found out about her. But they did. So, I had to tell them what I knew about Philip's whereabouts. It's funny though."

"What is?"

"They seemed to know about him being at Barnham. They kept asking where else. I didn't have a clue."

Dan thought for a while. "Who did Philip work for?"

"A cable company. They make cables for data transmission. Synchrony Communications."

"Did you call them?"

"Yes. They said Philip was involved in county-wide, Wi-Fi infrastructure planning. But they couldn't tell me how long it was going on for. They weren't very helpful."

"Well, they should know. Where are they based?"

"In Atlanta."

"Did you speak to Philip after he left for Barnham?"

"No. He said he was going to be back in a week, and it's now been 2 weeks. He doesn't call or answer his cell. I've emailed him, but he doesn't reply."

"And his work say they don't know here he is?"

"No. Apparently, he's left Barnham. He finished his work there, then just...vanished."

Dan did not say anything for a while. His spell was broken by Jody.

The older woman said, "It's not what you think."

"What am I thinking?"

"You're thinking there's another woman. Or there's gambling, drugs. But Philip wasn't like that. We were a happy family. Well, Tanya went off to college, but she visits all the time. Emory isn't far."

"Tell me about your daughter. What's her name?"

"Tanya. She's 21, at college in Emory. Doing a biology major."

"Does she know about her dad disappearing?"

"No. I don't want her to know either."

Dan said slowly, "Emory's a big college. Must be expensive, right?"

Jody wiped her eyes. "A cool 65 grand a year. Of which 47,300 grand is tuition fees. But she got a scholarship. She's a smart girl." Jody turned to look at Dan. "The only girl I have."

Dan tapped a finger on the steering wheel. He didn't want to say it, but he knew he had to. "Did Philip have money troubles? You know, for the tuition fees."

Jody held her forehead. "Oh, Jesus."

"Tell me," Dan said.

"The scholarship only covers half of the tuition fees. None of the living costs. She's our only child, right? Want to give her the best and all that. She had her heart set on that Biology major. One of the best in Georgia."

"Right," Dan said. He had no idea about biology majors.

Jody whispered, "I don't know if the fall semester fees have been paid yet."

"You can't check Philip's account?"

"No. He keeps the outgoings for the mortgage and tuition fees on a separate account. I don't have the password. He didn't have any savings plan for the college fees, I know that. He pays it every term."

Dan said, "So, if the fall fees are not paid..."

"They give her one term's grace, then she's out."

"When are the fees due?"

"This week."

Dan did some quick calculations in his head. He had a seven-figure sum left over from his Intercept final salary and bonus. And a house in Bethesda.

Dan asked, "You can ring the college and find out if the fees have been paid, can't you?"

Jody said, "Yes, I can. Why?"

"I can pay this semester's fees."

Jody's mouth fell open. She looked at Dan with wide eyes. "What?"

Dan said, "It's okay Jody. I can see you're in trouble here."

Jody shook her head. "No. I cannot let you do that, Dan."

"It's alright," Dan said.

Jody opened the car door and stepped out. "Thank you for offering, Dan. But I cannot accept that from someone I just met."

Jody walked over to the house. Dan locked the car and followed. Jody opened the front door slowly, like she expected something terrifying to happen. She stood silently for a while, then stepped inside. Dan walked in quickly behind her.

Jody was standing inside the living room. Her chest rose and fell, and her nostrils flared. She turned to Dan. He noticed the paleness of her face, skin stretched tight between the bones. Her dark blue eyes glazed over, and she blinked. Her straggly brown hair was pulled back in a ponytail.

Dan asked again, "Do you have any idea what they might be looking for, Jody?"

She moved her head from side to side. Dan could sense the torment in her. She was a strong woman, holding it in. She was determined not to let the panic overcome her. Slowly, she walked past Dan, into the hallway. Dan followed her into the kitchen. From there, upstairs. She couldn't bear standing in the bedroom. She ran down the stairs. Dan caught up with her at the base. Jody went into the kitchen, opened the bi fold doors with a set of keys, and stepped out into the garden.

The garden was more than forty feet in length. Pine trees rose up in the background, followed by a forest. Jody stepped off the patio and sat down. She lowered her head into her hands.

Dan said, "Let's get out of here."

Jody looked up. "Go where?"

Dan was looking into his phone. "There's a place downtown that we could visit."

Jody looked bewildered. "Like where?"

Dan smiled. "Lock up and let's get back in the car."

In fifteen minutes, Dan was pulling up at the grandiose entrance of the Ritz Carlton in downtown Atlanta. He chucked the keys to the valet. The valet stared dubiously at the car, but grinned when Dan pressed a twenty-dollar bill into his hand.

Jody was open mouthed again. She stuttered. "Dan, what…what the hell is this?"

Dan walked her to the concierge. He got a single room, and gave Jody the keys.

"This is where you'll be staying tonight."

Jody was shaking her head again. "No. No way. You hardly know me." She gave the keys back to Dan. "You can't do this."

Dan knew the type. She had morals. She had a sense of honor.

"Jody," he said quietly, "It's too dangerous for you to go back to that house tonight."

They had walked over to a table by the bar area. "What do you mean?" Jody asked.

"I mean, if I was them, and I knew that you were back in town, I would hit the house again tonight."

CHAPTER 8

It was early evening by the time Dan got back to Jody's house in Virginia Highland. He parked at the beginning of the avenue, more than a hundred meters from the house. Sunlight was fading but he could still see. He couldn't see a blue Chrysler anywhere on the road. After ten minutes, he drove up and parked in the driveway.

He let himself in with the key he had got from Jody. He shut the door and stopped. Something was biting away at the back of his mind and he realized what it was. There was no sign of a break in. Whoever had come in had entered with a set of keys.

Who did they get the keys from?

Dan took out his cell phone and a piece of paper. Jody had written down the number of Philip's employer.

Dan listened to the phone ring three times before a sing-song female voice picked up.

"Synchrony Communications. How can we help today?"

"I'm looking for a missing person who is an employee at your office."

Sing-song became downbeat, lost her rhythm. "Who is speaking?"

"I need to speak to the boss of Philip Longworth. You sent him out on a job a week ago, and now he's missing. Have the cops been?"

"Sir, I know nothing..."

"I'm sorry, I need to speak to your boss. Can you get him for me, please?"

"Hold on for a moment, sir."

Dan waited twenty seconds before a male voice came on the line. Deep set and heavy. "This is Marcus Schopp. Who is this?"

Dan explained everything.

Schopp listened without interruption, then said, "We win contracts to lay cables, Mr. Roy. That's why people get satellite TV in their homes. A new township is being built in Barnham and we are working there. Philip should be back anytime soon. He's a big boy, he can look after himself."

"So, someone from your office did report him as missing?"

Schopp grunted. "Yes, I believe so. He hadn't turned up for two days, so someone called the cops."

"How long was his assignment for?"

A slight hesitation. "Three days, I think." This man was the boss, Dan thought to himself. He should know how long Philip was down there for.

"Then doesn't it strike you as odd that he hasn't been home for more than two weeks? He's not called, not replied to his emails, or text."

"What do you want me to do, Mr. Roy? Hold his hand? Shall I spank him when he comes back, tell him not to do it again?"

A brief silence in which Dan could hear heavy breathing.

Schopp said, "I don't know what's bugging Philip, Mr. Roy. He's not done this before. I understand his wife and family are worried. For the record, cops say most missing men eventually come back on their own. Maybe you should just wait till he does so."

Schopp added, "Who are you, anyway?"

"A friend of the family."

"Alright, Mr. Roy, I think I have told you as much as I know. You still got questions, by all means, go to the cops." He hung up.

Dan picked his way around the destroyed house again. He had only cast a cursory glance at the third bedroom before. He went inside now. The walls were colored a light pink, and it looked like the girl's room. Tanya Longworth. She must have all her stuff at college, because there wasn't much in the wardrobes which had been opened and trashed. Dan lifted up the ripped carpet and checked underneath the floorboards, like he had with the other rooms.

Nothing. If there was, then it was probably taken by the men who had already been.

Downstairs a stack of bills caught his eye. The logo said Carter Medical Center. The invoice wasn't itemized, but they were stamped in red as being unpaid— twenty grand worth of unpaid medical bills. He made a note of the address of Carter Medical Center. He found a photo from a broken frame.

Tanya, Jody and Philip in happier days. They were dressed in anoraks and hiking gear. There was a blue sea sparkling behind them and they were on a white sandy hill. Somewhere on the coast, probably in Georgia. There was another photo of Philip in the same place, blue sea, same white sandy dune. It was close enough to see his face well. Dan put both photos in his pocket.

He was about to turn away from the main hallway when from the side of his eyes he caught a flicker of movement outside. A patrol car. Police. Atlanta PD. The car didn't flash its lights or sound the siren. Two half sleeved blue uniformed policemen got out and slammed the doors shut, heading straight for the house.

CHAPTER 9

There wasn't much time to think. It had to be one of the neighbors who called them. Dan would have to present himself as a family friend. They might not believe him, and maybe arrest him on the spot. There was one way of avoiding that. He strode to the front door and flung it open. The two uniforms coming up the drive stopped short, their hands reaching for the guns on their belts.

"Hello," Dan said, his face impassive. He filled up the doorway with his wide bulk. It would put them off, he thought. He stood to one side, holding the door open for them and nodded.

"Come in, please."

It was a man and a woman. Both young patrollers. They looked at each other, keeping their hands on their weapons.

"I'm a friend of the woman who lives in this house. Jody Longworth. Her husband's missing. I came down to check on the house."

The man asked, "What's your name?"

"Dan Roy." He waited for a second. "Look, if it bugs you that much, I can step outside while you have a look inside the house. It's been trashed."

The man whispered something to his partner. She nodded and stared at Dan.

"After you," the officer said. Dan could see the man's badge. The uniform and car looked genuine. He didn't like the idea of a man with a gun coming up behind him, but he needed to put this guy at ease.

"Okay," he said. He walked down the hallway, into the living room, the patrolman behind him.

"Jesus Christ," the officer said. Dan said nothing. He let the man observe for a few minutes, then took him round to the open plan kitchen area. Dan tested the bi-folding doors, then leaned against them. He let the man take his time, seeing the mess.

"Upstairs is similar," Dan said.

"You stay here. I'm going up to check."

Dan shrugged and fiddled with the lock of the bi-folding patio doors. It was open. He stepped out into the garden. The humidity seeped inside the broken space. Dan used his sleeve to wipe the sweat off his forehead. He heard a sound and looked back to see both cops in the dining room with their guns drawn. Double hands on their weapons, elbows extended, pointed straight at him. The man did the talking.

"You need to come with us to the station. You can come of your own volition or we'll have to arrest you."

"I got some questions myself. Can I lock up here first?"

"No," the cop said. "Keep your hands where we can see them. My partner will lock up."

Dan waited as the woman walked past him to the patio door. The man kept his gun trained on Dan.

Dan said, "I need to set the alarm too. You can't do that, and I'm not giving you the password."

The cop frowned. "We can set the alarm. It's not a problem. Give us the password."

Dan stood very still, his face impassive. "No."

The cop's face changed. He tightened the grip on his gun. "Then leave the alarm. We can lock the front door."

Dan said, "Listen to me. Whoever came in to wreck this place had keys for the door. The alarm could not have been set, or it would have gone off. Or they had the code for the alarm as well, I don't know. Either way, setting the alarm is not going to hurt. I need to do it."

The cop began to sweat. Dan waited, cool as a cucumber. The woman came around and whispered in her partner's ear. He took a deep breath, then nodded.

"OK," the cop said. The collar of his blue uniform was damp. "Just watch it. I don't want to shoot you. But I might have to."

Dan wanted to put the young guy at his ease. But he knew his words would not matter. Cops were the same the world over. But to their credit, they had given him the option of coming to the station of his own free will. That was better than an arrest.

Not the ideal way to begin a holiday. But he had faced far worse situations.

The guy covered him from the back, while the woman went outside the front door and watched him from the porch. Dan noticed she had not drawn her weapon, but kept her hand on it lightly. Less strung up than her partner.

Once Dan had set the alarm, he waited for the woman to lock the door. Then he stretched his hands out. "Keys, please," he said.

The male cop was between them in a flash. "No," he said. "First we need to take a statement off you at the station. If charges are placed against you, then you might not get the keys back."

The man was getting tiresome. But Dan kept his thoughts to himself. He turned on his heels and walked up to the police car.

It was a blue Ford Taurus. There was an extra stick out bumper at the front and back. It was black with Atlanta PD written on it in red letters. On the side of the car it said the same thing, with two extra words in white paint. Police Interceptor. LED flashlights on top. Dan leaned against the side, next to the rear doors.

The young cop came up, raised his eyebrows at him, and opened the door. Dan got in and the door slammed shut. It was hot, stuffy inside, with the smell of old leather. They got in at the front, and drove off slowly.

Dan lowered his window. It smelled of pine trees and fresh earth. They drove out of the neighborhood, and headed south, towards downtown. They used the backroads, and stopped in front of a red brick building that said "Atlanta Police Department Zone 1".

He was led to the front counter, where he had to give his name, address and ID. The officer checked his ID, looked interested and checked Dan out. Dan kept his eyes on the man without saying a word. He put his ID back in his pocket and walked to the reception area. He sat for ten minutes, then was called by the female cop who had come to the house. He followed her down a corridor into an interrogation room on the left. She knocked and entered. When Dan entered the room, she went out and shut the door.

CHAPTER 10

The room had whitewashed walls, a metal table with the legs screwed into the floor and two fold up metal chairs on either side. Two suits sat at the table. One of them stood. He had light sandy hair, a lined face that had seen better days, and wore an open collar suit that hung loose on him. He flashed his badge.

"I'm Detective Brown, and this is Detective Harris." Harris nodded. "Sit down, Mr. Roy."

Dan sat, facing the two detectives. Harris looked sharper. He was younger, mid-thirties, with busy dark eyes that looked Dan up and down.

Harris said, "You are Daniel Roy, is that right?"

"Yes."

Harris looked at a paper in his hand. "From Bethesda, Virginia. Says here US Army. You used to be in the Delta Forces, but that was seven years ago." Harris put the papers down. "Where have you been all this time, Mr. Roy?"

"Been abroad. With work."

Harris said, "What sort of work?"

Killing people. Blowing up compounds. Stopping the US Embassy from getting bombed sky high.

That kind of work.

Dan said, "Jody Longworth is a friend of mine. Her house was ransacked and her husband's disappeared. She wants to know why."

There was a knock at the door. The female officer poked her head in. She said, "A file on Philip Longworth." Harris took the file from her hands and thanked her.

Dan waited while the two men read the file. He asked, "Any news?"

Harris said, "If you mean any viewings or sighting matching his description, then no. We know that his credit card was used to purchase a return ticket to Barnham from Atlanta Rail Station. Card's not been used

38

after that. Barnham PD has no records of him."

"Hotel registrations? Car rentals? In Barnham, I mean. He's there for work. Has to be eating, drinking somewhere."

"Must be using cash, Mr. Roy." Dan thought about the bank statement he had seen in Philip's study. It didn't look like the man had a load of cash at his disposal.

"Any cash withdrawals from his bank account?"

"Nope. We checked. Checked with his employer as well. No issues there."

"Are you putting out an APB?"

Harris sighed and looked at his colleague. Brown stayed reclined in his seat, like all of this was an effort. But his eyes examined Dan closely.

"An All-Points Bulletin is for people who are missing for prolonged periods, Mr. Roy. Not two weeks. He's probably soaking up some rays somewhere. Found a friend. I don't know. We see this a lot. Middle-aged man, needs a break from life. He should be back soon."

"How long is soon?"

Brown shrugged. "A month, maybe two."

"You know the house was trashed. Someone used a fine toothcomb, searching for something. That doesn't bother you?"

Harris said, "That's new evidence. Yes, we have to evaluate the case in that light now, but there's no plan of putting out an APB."

The other detective, Andy Brown, turned to Dan. "How did you meet Jody Longworth this time?"

Dan considered his response, then said, "At the airport. She was coming back from New Jersey." Dan had already asked Jody this. She had been to Nutley, NJ, to see her friend. She had caught the flight back from Newark when she bumped into Dan at Atlanta airport.

Dan said, "The front door was locked. The windows hadn't been forced. The bi-folding doors at the back were open. Maybe whoever came in had to leave quickly. They definitely had keys. They left via the garden. When Jody and I came back, we might even have surprised them. There's a pine forest at the back. They escaped through there."

He waited for the detectives to digest this. Dan continued, "Maybe that's what the neighbor saw. Someone running out the back. Or he or she got worried that two strange men were entering via the front door."

The two officers were holding something back. Dan knew it.

"Who did the neighbor see?" Dan persisted. The two cops stared back at him.

"I'm not a suspect, am I?" Dan asked. Harris looked at Brown again, who shrugged.

"Alright Mr. Roy," Harris said. "The neighbor saw a tall, Caucasian male enter the building this morning. With a group of four men. About three hours before your arrival. Yes, they did see the same guys run out the back as well, just when you arrived."

"What was the tall guy wearing?"

Harris looked at his notes again. "A black shirt and dark brown pants. Blond hair. Big guy."

A tall, white man wearing dark clothes. The description matched the man Dan had seen at the airport. The man who kidnapped Jody.

"Thank you," Dan said. "Did the neighbors hear an alarm going off?"

Brown said, "Not that we heard of."

Dan asked, "Were the other men with the tall guy Hispanic? Or Mexican?"

Harris said, "Yes. One of the neighbors mentioned that."

Brown said, "Where is Jody Longworth now?"

"Somewhere safe."

Harris leaned forward. "Let me remind you something here, Mr. Roy. You are in a police station, and you are giving a statement. You do understand, right?"

Dan did not reply. Harris continued. "That being the case, some cooperation would be in order."

Dan said, "This was an inside job. Someone had Philip's keys. Probably knew the alarm key code as well. Philip would not just hand them over. He might have been tortured. This is not about me. We need to find Philip."

Brown asked, "And what brings you to Atlanta?"

Dan said, "Like I said, I had work overseas. Running a business. I came to

Atlanta on holiday. Just happened to bump into Jody at the airport."

"Just like that?"

"Yup."

"So where is she now?"

After a pause, Dan said, "In a hotel downtown. She'll be safe there."

Brown said, "I'm not a fool, Mr. Roy. I know for sure that you have an angle here. I don't know what you are playing at, or what authority you have. Are you working for the FBI?"

Dan smiled. Not wanting to work for a giant bureaucracy was exactly the reason he had left the Army in the first place. "No. I'm definitely not working for the FBI."

The two detectives seemed to relax at his answer. There was a knock at the door, and the female cop returned with a folder. She whispered something in Harris' ears then went out.

Harris scraped his chair back. All three stood up. Brown extended his hand.

"Here's my card. Call me if you think of anything."

"Nice to meet you, Detective Brown."

Dan shook his hand, feeling the hard grip. He shook hands with Harris and walked out.

CHAPTER 11

North Atlantic Ocean
268 miles east of Jacksonville, Georgia, USA
East of US continental shelf

Captain Mikhail Shevchenko gripped the railings on the foredeck of the *Nimika* and stared out at the ocean. The research vessel was on its maiden voyage. The sun was out and seagulls scoured the clear skies overhead. He patted the railings affectionately. He had waited seven long years for this ship to be built at the Yantar shipyard in Kaliningrad on the Baltic Sea. As yet, there was no other ship like it.

Ships such as the *Nimika* had to be sturdy, often battling with severe conditions including gales and cyclones. This ship was virtually unsinkable and had satellite locators which, when activated, fed its location with pin-point precision to patrolling Russian ships on the African coast. Its GPS signal was on a frequency that couldn't be jammed. But that wasn't why the *Nimika* was special.

It had the next generation of sonar screens to pick up very low frequencies, and the latest biological sensors to find even a few molecules of radioactive waste a nuclear submarine might leave behind. By virtue of its two bow thrusters it could achieve speeds of eighteen knots, unheard-of for a heavy research vessel. The ship dragged a load of sonar screens on a platform behind it, and on the stern there was a white dome-shaped sonar receiver that looked like a giant golf ball.

Shevchenko patted his beard and moved aft, spreading his legs to adjust against the swell. He spent a few seconds there, then walked back towards the bridge. Behind and above the bridge was a helipad, but the Kremlin's machinations meant he wasn't allowed a helicopter on this voyage. Still, he had something far more powerful at his disposal.

In the bridge, the young OR-5 Sergeant, as junior Petty Officers in the Russian Navy were known, put down his binoculars and saluted when he saw Shevchenko enter.

"Good morning, Alexeyivich," Shevchenko murmured, taking up position next to him. Alexander Alexeyivich, known as Sasha, was a graduate of the Kuznetsov Naval Academy. The same Academy in St Petersburg from which every Russian naval officer graduated, including Shevchenko himself.

"Beautiful weather today, Captain," Sasha said.

"Yes indeed," Shevchenko mumbled. He turned around and headed down the spiral staircase to the ship's main body. Sasha, aware of his master's moods, followed without comment. They descended into the heart of the ship where in a large dry dock, taking up almost half the size of the interior, lay their two most prized possessions.

Shevchenko walked forward and patted the hull of the 20 feet long, and 1400-pound heavy large submersible carried in a cradle, attached to the slings of a crane, ready for lifting.

"Today would be a good day for it, Captain," Sasha said.

Shevchenko smiled to himself. The impetuousness of youth.

"Today would not be a good day for it, young Sasha, because we do not have all the information as yet. Do not lose sight of the mission objective." He looked up at the young man and raised his eyebrows. "But, it could be the day for a test run."

A smile appeared on Sasha's face. "Yes, sir."

Sasha put out a call on the intercom and crew members rushed into the dry dock. As Shevchenko watched, Sasha barked out orders and the men went through the drills. A groaning noise started and the crane tightened the rubber straps.

The men did a quick, last minute check on the sides of submersible, called the *Guboki*—Russian for "deep". Of particular importance to Shevchenko was the removable data storage module. He made sure it was secure, then stepped back. He nodded to Sasha and the men moved away.

The floor began to vibrate. A circular area in the middle began to recede, moving back all the way to reveal the ocean below. The cranes whined louder and the *Guboki* was lifted out of its cradle. It wobbled in the air slightly, then began to descend towards the water.

Shevchenko and Sasha returned to the bridge. The room adjacent had been set up as the control room for the submersible and two scientists were already there, fiddling with the keyboards, facing a large dashboard of screens. An acoustic monitor beeped occasionally.

One of them turned to Shevchenko. "What depth, Captain?"

Shevchenko thought to himself. The geophysical assessments of yesterday showed the depth of the sea bed to be almost 3000 meters. This was beyond the continental shelf and he was expecting four miles, so three wasn't bad. Time to push the *Guboki* to live up to its name—to go deep. It had withstood sea pressure of 4500 meters in its simulations.

"Descend to 1000 meters, comrade Pushkin."

Pushkin flicked buttons. "1000 meters, Captain. What speed?"

"Depends on the currents. They do not appear strong, but start with two-and-half knots." That was good for a machine of this size. The *Guboki* could achieve up to six knots.

Shevchenko said, "Gradually descend to the floor at 3000 meters approximately. Then surface at twenty kilometer intervals, just as a test to make sure it's all okay. Do a circle with a radius of seventy miles, then come back to base."

"Yes, Captain."

Sasha said excitedly, "Its test voyage in the Mediterranean lasted for five hundred miles and two hundred hours, Captain."

"Yes, Sasha," Shevchenko said patiently. "It travelled under a US Navy aircraft carrier and they did not even find it. I know that."

Sasha gulped. "What I meant, Comrade Captain, is that it should be easily able to complete this mission."

"No, Sasha," Shevchenko said. "This mission is more difficult. We do not know of American capabilities in these waters. That is why we need that information. It should be here soon. But hopefully before that, we can find what we are looking for."

"And then we can start?"

"Yes, we can start."

"With any luck, Captain, the effect will be a calamity for America."

Shevchenko suppressed a smile. These young guns were full of the new party bluster. In some ways, it reminded him of his younger days.

"With any luck, yes."

"Soveitski Syoz, Darogi Kapitan." To the Soviet Union, my dear Captain. A common Russian toast, tinted with nostalgia for greater days now firmly in the past.

"Sovietski Syoz, Maladoi Chelovek." To the Soviet Union, young man.

A young man indeed, Shevchenko thought. Lucky to be on such a revolutionary voyage.

CHAPTER 12

Dan got a ride back in the same patrol car. At the house, he walked around to the back and stood in the patio, then stepped into the garden. The long grass brushed against his ankles. He walked to the end where a waist-high fence separated the property from the pine forest beyond. He turned and looked back at the house. There was a balcony on the back bedroom as well. The sloped roof could have a loft conversion. He thought about that. He needed to check if there was a loft space. The men had been searching for something. He left everything else it seemed, apart from Philip's laptop.

Dan checked the garden. The dry turf, some of it bleached in the sun, didn't show anything. No footprints. No cartridge cases. No drops of blackened blood.

He went back inside and cleaned up the kitchen the best he could, then called a cab and headed out to the nearest supermarket.

He came back with some groceries and cut some fennel, onions and mushrooms. He turned on the oven and put them in. He raided the larder, it was well stocked. He took out the soy sauce and honey. There was a packet of pork chops in the fridge. He rubbed a honey and soy mixture on the meat and put them in the hot oven. Below the pork chops he put in the vegetables. He put the beer in the fridge.

He went upstairs and looked at the ceiling above the landing, and in each on the bedrooms. He went out on the balcony at the back. There was no access to the loft space above. He went to the balcony in the front bedroom, picking his way through the foam ripped up from the bed and the wardrobe doors on the floor. The telephone had been ripped off their sockets. He put his hands on the balcony and looked out. A couple was walking down the street.

Then he saw the blue Chrysler in the distance.

He wouldn't have seen it unless he'd looked carefully. He could see the front of the car, the driver and a passenger. There could be others in the back. Dan went back inside. It would be a dark in an hour, around 9:00 p.m.

Back in the kitchen he took out the pork chops, sprinkled rock salt and pepper from the dispenser. The fennel onions and mushroom were a bit well done, but edible. He ate on the table and washed it down with a beer. Thirty minutes had passed. He checked the back. The garden was empty.

He went upstairs and got one of Philip's old jackets, an anorak with multiple pockets. He put a long kitchen knife in the inside pocket and stuck a smaller one in his front belt. In the garden shed he found a hammer. It had a heavy metal head and a thick rubber grip. He put that into one of the anorak pockets. Outside it was still warm, the sky darkening with shades of pink and violet.

Another fifteen minutes, he figured. Maybe half an hour.

From the front bedroom, he could still see the blue Chrysler. With the curtains open, he put the lights on in the bedroom and the study. Then he went back downstairs and into the garden.

Dan crept down the side of the house and along the fence. He lay down flat on the ground, resting on the side entrance. The darkness grew around him. A car passed by, then silence returned to the street.

He heard the engine before he saw anything.

Lights off, the Chrysler came slowly up to the front of the house. Four men got out, closing the doors gently. Light streamed on them from the bedroom above and Dan could make out their faces. All of them looked Hispanic. The driver seemed to be the leader. He had tattoos on his arms and neck, and a piercing on his eyebrow. He took a gun out and released the safety. Dan crept farther back, then threw himself down in a plant bed, crawling under the bushes. One man approached the garden from the side. He walked out to the patio, took out a handgun and looked around. Someone knocked on the bi-folding doors and he spun around, gun raised. He relaxed when he saw one of his own and waved.

Dan kept his head down as the man in the garden stepped off the patio onto the grass. He came towards the plants. Dan kept very still. He could barely see. The footsteps stopped two meters away. Dan could hear the man shuffle closer. He tensed his muscles. Had he seen something? Maybe Dan's trunks, sticking out the back? Dan heard another shuffling sound, and then more footsteps. But fading now.

Silently, Dan uncoiled himself.

He raised himself to his knees, staying low. The hammer came out. He hefted the heavy object in his hand. The knife would kill the man, but he might fight first. The hammer was better. Dan crept out, following. The man had no idea. He was looking ahead, towards the garden shade. When he was close, Dan charged, hitting the side of the man's face and hearing the cheekbone crack. As the man fell, Dan grabbed his neck and jumped on top of him. He raised the hammer high up and smashed it down on the side of the temple, where important blood vessels travelled up the side of the ear. It was the best place to hit someone on the skull. Another crunching sound. The body jerked once, then was still. Dan felt for the gun on the grass. A Glock 22. He released the breech and the magazine dropped out. He couldn't see in the dark, but he was pretty sure it was a fifteen-round magazine. It wasn't suppressed.

He left the body and stole out to the side entrance. He put the Glock in a pocket and held the hammer in his hand. He spread-eagled himself on the floor. The Chrysler was in front of him, and leaning against the side he could see the silhouette of a man.

That meant two were inside the house. The light in the bedroom above had been turned off. The man at the car was facing the house, and his left side was turned slightly away from Dan. He probably had his gun out. It was safer to assume that. Dan couldn't use his weapon. It would make too much noise. Besides, he wanted at least one of them alive and to use some field interrogation techniques on the survivor. Make him talk, before he died.

With this guy, Dan had one problem. He was jammed between the car and the side entrance. It was an awkward space to navigate, if he had to get up to the man undetected. Dan crouched forward on one knee like a sniper. He had a clear view of the man's head from the side. He threw the hammer as hard as he could. At the same time, he moved. The hammer smashed into the man's head just as Dan slammed into the man's waist, trapping him against himself and the car. Dan frantically fell for the man's hand, searching for a gun. There was no need. The hammer had found its target and the man crumpled to the ground. He was dazed, and Dan hit him again, in the same spot on the temple.

He looked up towards the house and saw a flashlight briefly in the study. He stepped over the prostrate body and went to the door. It was ajar. He sank to his knees and looked in. Completely dark. He stayed in that position and heard a whispered voice from near the staircase.

Then the creaking of stairs. They were coming down.

CHAPTER 13

Dan sank down low. The door opened. One man stepped out, then another. Dan didn't give them a chance to see the dead man. He brought the hammer up with savage ferocity, aiming for the side of the man's face in front of him. There was a thud, a grunt, and the blow almost lifted the smaller man off his feet. Dan was charging, heading low for the man in front, probably the leader. He cannoned into the man just as he was turning to find out what happened behind him.

He stumbled and fell forward, and Dan spread his legs to sit astride his back. The man's gun arm was caught underneath him. Dan took out the Glock and pushed it against the man's ear.

"*Que pasa, hombre?* Move and you die. Who sent you?"

The man's cheek was squashed against the floor. He spoke between his teeth. "Fuck you."

"Wrong answer."

Dan leaned on the man's head with his arm. He caught a whiff of stale sweat and cannabis. He hooked his hand around and used his fingers like claws to dig inside the man's eyes. The man shouted something in Spanish and thrashed around. Dan realized he couldn't do this in the open. He needed to drag the man inside. He grabbed his collar and lowered his voice.

"I am going to let you stand up. If you don't do as I tell you, then I will blow your brains out. Do you understand?"

"Yes."

"Give me your gun. Take your arm out slowly." He pushed the pistol harder against the man's skull. The man moved his arm out from below him. He did it slowly. Dan twisted his neck to watch him. He had raised his foot, ready to kick the gun hand, if needed. When the gun was fully out the man suddenly cocked his wrist, aiming at Dan. He wasn't fast enough. Dan's trunk slammed down on the hand and the round went up into the sky. The shot ran out, echoing against the houses. Dan hit the man with the butt of the Glock. Two hefty blows on the mastoid bone at the back of the ears and the man was still.

The guy who was first out the door hadn't moved. All four down.

Dan dragged all the bodies inside the house, put the lights on and searched them. They all had tattoos. He ripped open the shirt of one. Lots more tattoos on the chest and trunk, many with Spanish inscriptions. Down the middle, Z9 written in large letters. A street gang, with a penitentiary chapter, more than likely.

Dan called Detective Brown. He picked up at the second ring.

"Detective Brown speaking."

Dan explained what had happened. Fifteen minutes later, an unmarked police car pulled up outside the house. Brown was wearing his suit and he had a flashlight. Dan opened the door for him. Brown had his Glock raised. He lowered it when he saw Dan.

"This their car?" Brown indicated the Chrysler. Dan nodded.

Brown followed Dan into the kitchen. He looked at the bodies, then at Dan. "Jesus Christ, you did this?"

"Self-defense," Dan said. "It was me or them."

Brown kneeled down and looked at the tattoos. He put a finger on their necks to feel for a pulse. "Jesus Christ," he said again.

"What is Z9?" Dan asked.

"Zapato 9. Named after their leader, Zapato Mares, now locked up in El Salvador." Brown looked up. "These guys are all over the place. Up and down the country." He stood up.

"Drugs, extortion, what else?"

"They're big on human trafficking as well. Sell Mexican girls as slaves. Cocaine, too. Those are their two main businesses—cocaine and prostitution." Brown shook his head. "If Longworth was mixed up with them, then it's bad news."

"You reckon Philip was selling for them on the side? I can't see him being mixed up with prostitution."

Brown let out a long breath. "How do you know? A middle-class white guy in the 'burbs is exactly the kind of guy these gangs want to act as a front for them. It's happened before. Mainly with narcotics, but you would be surprised of the filthy shit we uncover sometimes."

"They want something from him."

"Money, probably."

"What doesn't figure is the tall blond guy."

"No, it doesn't. But don't forget these gangs operate here because there's demand. They deal in weapons, they act as enforcers for biker gangs and organized crime families. So the blond guy is mixed up with them. I bet you."

"No one matching his description ever been on your radar?"

"Not that I recall. But the Mexican gangs, especially these guys, have become more active in Atlanta recently. They use the city as a major transit route for cocaine they bring in from Peru and El Salvador, via Texas. The business had died down, but now it's up and running again."

Dan said, "Can you clear this up for me?"

Brown was silent for a while, then nodded. "This changes everything. Now we have new angles. Might have to get the FBI involved as well."

"Or the DEA." Dan ran his hand through his hair. This was getting worse.

"Yes," Brown said shortly. "I'm calling an ambulance. We can say they were trying to rob an empty house. You got back late and found them inside. You acted in self-defense. But this becomes a crime scene now. The lab guys will come around to do their thing."

He looked at Dan. "What are you gonna do?"

"I need to check out the employer."

Brown felt inside his pant pockets. There was a film of sweat on his brow. He pulled out a packet of Marlboro cigarettes and headed outside the folding doors of the kitchen. He lit a cigarette, took a deep drag and blew out smoke.

After a pause, Dan joined him outside.

Brown offered him the pack. "Smoke?"

Dan said, "No thanks. You alright?"

Brown swallowed and said, "Yeah, fine." He cracked a smile. "See dead bodies all the time, right? Sometimes it's like half of this city is dying."

Brown smoked in silence for a while. "What did you do before you joined Delta?" he asked.

Dan said, "US Ranger."

Brown smiled. "A Bat Boy, huh?"

"A proud one as well. Why do you wanna know?"

"Ex-US Army. Airborne as well. 82nd Airborne Division."

Dan nodded. The 82nd Airborne Division had been deployed all over the world. They played a major role in all combat theaters, and were also based at Fort Bragg, NC, where Dan had been billeted during his Delta years.

"I knew you were a tough guy when I saw you," Brown said. "You don't fit the bill of a regular army grunt."

Dan kept his voice gentle. "You get those dreams? Flashbacks?"

Brown took another lung full of smoke. "Used to. Got past it, now."

"That why you left the Army?"

Brown kept his eyes averted from Dan and nodded. "Kind of. You know what it's like, right?"

"Yeah. Never had it myself, but I know others." After a beat, Dan said, "But you're gonna be OK, man. You're holding down a job, doing well for yourself."

Brown took a deep drag. "Some ain't so lucky, right?"

"Right." Dan turned to leave. Brown called him.

"Dan."

Dan stopped. "Yeah?"

"Thanks, dude."

Dan nodded. Only soldiers knew what it was like. Combat left scars on the mind. Scars no one could see. And professional soldiers were expected to settle down to civilian life like nothing had happened. Like Brown said, some were not so lucky.

Brown called after Dan, "You be careful out there. I don't like what's happening here."

"That which does not kill me," Dan said, "makes me stronger."

CHAPTER 14

After Brown left, the crime scene guys arrived. They set up tape around the house, put on their white suits and got to work. Dan found himself a corner in one of the bedrooms upstairs and tried to catch some sleep. Before he turned in, he rang Jody and brought her up to speed. He promised he would come and see her the next day, and told her not to leave the hotel. He didn't forget to take her daughter's cell number.

Dan was up and out early the next morning.

He walked past the World of Coca Cola and down the steps of the Centennial Olympic Park. The fountain was sprouting high and he caught some spray as he walked close. He preferred to walk. The heat was sapping, even at 10:00 a.m. He had a baseball cap on, and sunglasses. No one followed him. He headed south, looking for a road called Edgewood Avenue. He found it after another ten minutes, guided by his phone.

The avenue had a tramline on the left strip and cars on the right. He needed number 1430. The building turned out to be a single floor, blue-tinted glass and metallic structure opposite a faded red brick Victorian building. A curious juxtaposition of the old and new. Commercial buildings lined the road, but next to the Victorian building there was a modern two-story structure with Greek letters in a pediment on top. Probably an off-campus sorority house. There was a parking lot next to it, with Fords and BMW's closest to the street.

Number 1430 looked average, nothing special. There was no street entry door and it took him a while to find it around the back. There was a parking lot, and next to it, an entrance to the building. Dan stopped. The guard at the doorway looked heavy. He was standing still, feet planted apart. He wore a black baseball cap, black fatigues and a bullet-proof Kevlar vest. A Heckler and Koch MP5 submachine gun was held loosely in his hands, but his finger was on the trigger. He saw Dan coming and the MP5 came up, barrel pointing straight at Dan. The butt was against his midriff, but he was comfortable. Dan knew a sniper when he saw one. This was no ordinary security guard.

"Yes?" the guard asked.

"I am here to see Marcus Schopp. The boss."

"Stop there," the guard called. Dan did. The MP5 barrel lifted until the man had it on a shoulder stance, pointed straight at Dan's head.

"What do you want from him?"

"I'm a friend of Philip Longworth. He's missing, and the cops are coming here after me. They have some questions for Mr. Schopp."

The gun didn't go down. Dan heard a sound behind him and he turned around. Another gun barrel. Same weapon. H&K MP5. This guard was wearing a similar black uniform, baseball cap, and he was less than five feet away from Dan. Close enough for Dan to see the weapon was switched to automatic mode. A squeeze on the trigger would literally blow Dan away.

"Against the wall. *Now.*"

Dan turned around and raised his hands. Hands pushed him against the wall. He spread his legs. These guys would ask him to, if he didn't. He could guess who they were. Ex Rangers or Delta, maybe even Seals, now working as private military contractors. The hands frisked him and up down expertly.

"Turn around," the guard said.

Dan turned to see both guns aimed straight at his chest. The men stared at Dan without blinking. One of them went to the intercom and buzzed. He looked back at Dan. "What's the name?"

"Dan Roy."

The guard spoke in a low voice at the intercom. Then he turned to his colleague and nodded. The second man indicated with his gun, and moved towards the double doors.

Dan walked past them and through the double doors that had swung open silently. He was in a brightly lit white hallway. There was no reception desk and he didn't know which way to turn. There were wooden framed photos of suspension bridges and cables.

A woman in nice white shoes walked past him and he caught her eye.

Pretty. Smoky green eyes, five eight, navy blue skirt suit trimmed around the bust and waist, accentuating her figure. Dark hair, falling in waves at the shoulder. She smiled and Dan smiled back. He kept his eyes on her as she walked to the end of the hallway and turned a corner without looking back at him.

"Mr. Roy." Another woman, older this time, with a bowed back, was waiting for him. A man in a similar black uniform to the guards outside was standing behind her. He kept his steely eyes on Dan, and Dan stared back at him as he walked up. He was holding a Heckler and Koch 416 assault rifle. Dan's weapon of choice. The H&K handgun was strapped to the right thigh, the extra ammunition in the center of the chest piece. Another hand gun at the left waistline. These guys were well-equipped, and more than normal security. Dan following the woman down the hallway. They went through another set of double doors and into a waiting room.

"Have a seat here, please. I will let Mr. Schopp know that you have arrived."

He knew already, Dan thought. He nodded and sat down. He picked up a copy of the *Atlanta Gazette*. The Democratic Party's computers had been hacked. Confidential emails between senators leaked out, including many between supposed rivals on the other side. Republican senators were quick to fault the Democrat's cyber systems and were denying all knowledge of the emails. Politics.

The circus continued, with the best jokers in the nation. Or worst jokers, depending how you saw it. Financed by the tax dollars of millions of hard working Americans.

"Mr. Schopp will see you now," the secretary announced.

Dan stood up and followed her. The office was spacious, more photos of cabling and engineering projects on the walls. His feet sank in the carpet. A series of tall windows at the back lit the room up.

Next to the windows, at a huge mahogany desk, sat a man who could be summed up in one word—round. Marcus Schopp was in his sixties, with a round face, bald round scalp and rounded shoulders. He stepped out from behind the desk and Dan saw the prominent gut, held up by two small legs.

He looked like a large penguin in a black suit. They stared at each other for a while.

"You are Philip's friend?" Schopp asked in that gravelly voice that Dan heard on the phone.

"Yes."

Schopp made a noise in his throat that was between a growl and a choke. He curled his lips up in disdain, like Dan had somehow brought a bad smell into the room.

"I told you on the phone. I have nothing else to add."

"How about turning Philip's house inside out, searching it with a fine toothcomb, then sending four Latino gang members around?"

The corners of Schopp's eyes crinkled. For an instant, there was a lack of control. Rage. Then it was gone.

"What the hell are you talking about?"

Dan told him. Schopp's black eyes stayed focused on Dan, giving nothing away. Dan could see other movements. His thumb on the desk kept rubbing against his forefinger. His ankle twitched up and down. All the signs of a nervous man.

"Tell me about Philip," Dan said.

Schopp rolled his eyes. "This is a rat's ass, you know that? What do you want, a character reference?"

"What I told you just now makes no difference? I want to know what he was like the days before he went off to Barnham. How he acted. Did he come to see you?"

"Hell, no. I don't have time to see all my employees. Look, if he's mixed up in something bad with these gangs, that's his problem. Not mine, and not my company's."

"He had money worries. Mortgage and college fees. How much was he being paid?"

"That's confidential information."

"You couldn't have been paying him much. He was way in the red in his checking account."

"Like I said. Get his bank statements and find out."

Dan tried a different tack. "Tell me about Barnham."

Schopp sighed. "Again, like I said…"

"Laying cables for Wi-Fi across the county, I know that," Dan interrupted. "He got a one-way ticket to there. Didn't seem like he was coming back in a hurry."

"And?"

"Why would he do that?"

"I don't know." The look on his face was stubborn. Dan wouldn't get anywhere like this. Marcus Schopp knew something, but either he was scared to tell him, or didn't want to.

"You are next, Schopp. They're coming after you," Dan said softly.

Schopp's face turned purple. "Get out!" he shouted.

Dan turned on his heels and left.

CHAPTER 15

Dan came out of the office, walked through the empty waiting area and into the open hallway. The hallway was empty. Dan looked around him. The corridor bent round the corners on either side, the building was in the shape of a doughnut. In front of him there was a door. Behind, steps going down to what seemed like the basement.

Dan went through and down the stairs, coming to a corridor that was a replica of the one above. Here a white door had a small glass window near the top. He looked inside. Rows of computer screens with a few people hunched over them. The door didn't have a handle, only a retina screening machine and, next to it, a larger device in the shape of a human hand. A *Vein map*.

Dan had seen these before in the CIA office in Langley, and also at the Intercept office. Fingerprints could be forged, but no two individuals had the same pattern of veins in their hands.

He moved on. A door on the opposite side was a janitor's cabinet. The corridor was empty. Dan opened the cabinet door. There was a small space inside it. He shut the door, and turned the light on. Inside, a uniform hung on the wall. He put it on quickly. Luckily the janitor was a big man. He took out a broom and bucket, filled the bucket with water, and dragged them out into the corridor.

He walked around in a circle. The room with the white door took up a lot of the ground floor. On his left he found a door that opened into a hallway. At the end - two offices. The place was empty. Dan put the broom and bucket against the wall. He took out a piece of cloth and started to rub the windows.

He could see the security camera above the door as he came in. He got a chair and stood on it. A wide-angle lens. Keeping his face hidden below the camera, he took out the black glass cover. It was a screw top. He tied the piece of cloth around the camera lens. Then he screwed the cover back on. He got off the chair and put it back in place.

The office doors did not have any signs on them. Dan tried one. It was open. The room was dark. He turned the light on revealing a table with a laptop in the middle and a larger screen to one side. He went to the table.

Two folders on the top. Both were stamped Classified, USN. US Navy. Dan opened the folders. Numbers, diagrams and flowcharts that he would have to read through.

He flipped out his cell phone and started taking pictures. When he finished, he opened up the laptop. He needed a password. He looked around the room. Two filing cabinets behind the table. He was going to move towards it when he stopped short.

Two male voices. Heading for the office. Dan went to the wall and turned the light off. He stole back to the filing cabinets. Behind them there was an alcove against the wall. Dan pressed against it and sank down to his knees.

The door handle turned, then stopped. He could hear the voices clearly now and one of them belonged to Marcus Schopp. He stopped at the entrance of the door, speaking to someone outside.

"He says he's a friend, but how do you know? I mean, how the hell do you know? He could be anyone," Schopp's voice was frustrated. The person at the other end said something.

"Yeah, you gotta be careful. I'll see you upstairs." Schopp said, and came inside the room.

He flicked the light switch on. Dan drew his knees closer and breathed as softly as possible.

There was a creaking sound and a grunt as Schopp sat down in the leather chair. He rustled the papers in the folder. Then Dan heard the sound of the chair being shoved back. Padded footsteps approached the filling cabinet.

Dan flexed his jaws. His knuckles were white. The cabinet was six doors tall and he could see Marcus's shoes around the corner.

He was standing on his tiptoes. Marcus said something to himself, took some papers out of the cabinet, then slammed the cabinet shut. He went back to the table. Dan breathed. Marcus picked up the files and went to the door. He flicked off the lights and left.

Dan crawled out from behind the filing cabinet.

He let his eyes get used to the dark, then tried the top drawer. It was locked. He looked at the table. Marcus had taken the folders. He went to the door and put his ear against it. Silence. He opened the door a crack. The reception area was empty. He got his broom and bucket off the wall and went back to the janitor's cupboard. He passed the white door and glanced in again. The same people were sat there, eyes focused intently on the screen. One of the screens facing Dan had a map of USA with flashing lights on the east and west coast.

Dan turned away. He changed quickly in the janitor's cupboard and made his way back to the upstairs corridor.

He walked straight into the same woman he had seen earlier in the hallway. Sea green, smoky eyes, nice blue dress and very attractive.

"Just been to see Marcus?" she asked.

Dan kept his face impassive. "Who wants to know?"

"Lisa Chandler." She extended her hand. She smelled of lavender and sandalwood. Her hair was dark chestnut, and it contrasted with her light eyes watching him, moving from his chest to his shoulders.

"Dan Roy." They shook hands.

"You work here?" Dan asked.

"Yup. I needed to see Marcus myself, but was told he has a visitor. Guess that must have been you."

"Yes. He's free now."

Lisa shrugged. "It makes no difference really. He's always in a bad mood. Luckily, he leaves us alone most of the time."

"You been here long?"

"Coming up to five years. Yeah, it feels long."

"You might have known my friend. Guy called Philip Longworth."

Lisa frowned. "You know Philip?"

"Yes, he's been missing for a week now, so I'm helping my aunt look for him."

Lisa's eyes flicked behind Dan. He guessed a guard was moving up behind him.

Dan said "These guards always around?"

"Uh-huh. More in the last six months. There's two more on the other side."

"Why does a cable company need security like this?"

"We do a lot of work for the DoD. Military applications."

"Fair enough. But these aren't any ordinary guards."

Lisa nodded. She dropped her voice. "I'm on my lunch break. Do you want to go for a quick coffee?"

"Sure, let's do that."

CHAPTER 16

Lisa knew a place behind the Centennial Olympic Park. The sun was high and the heat was like a haze around them. Dan had bought a pair of handkerchiefs on his way down. He felt like he needed a towel.

Lisa watched him wipe his forehead. "Not used to the heat, huh?"

"You could say that. It's more the humidity, actually," he added.

"Are you from around here?"

"From Virginia, originally. But spent a lot of time abroad. When I was a kid, I lived with my parents in Nepal."

"You lived in Nepal?"

"Yes. You know where Nepal is?"

She looked at him like he had asked a stupid question. "Mountain kingdom in the Himalayas, north of India. Capital Kathmandu. Favorite haunt of the hippies in the sixties. Best trekking in the world and white-water rafting. That Nepal?"

Dan pressed his lips together. "Alright, I'm sorry. Guess you know about Nepal. We lived in a Gurkha village. My dad trained me in physical labor like the Gurkha kids."

"The Gurkhas are a warrior tribe aren't they? The fought for the British, I think."

"They still do. Five regiments in the Brigade of Gurkhas. We left when I was sixteen and came back to Virginia." Dan did not want to say anything more.

Lisa asked "And then?"

"Joined the Army. Saw the world."

He could feel Lisa's eyes on his face. She wanted more elaboration from him, he could tell. But Dan did not speak to anyone about his life in the Army and thereafter.

They found a café and sat down. It was lunchtime and workers with their lunch boxes and takeout food were slowly filling the park. It was school holidays and some kids ran around, playing tag. Dan ordered a caramel macchiato and Lisa got herself a skinny latte.

He asked, "How well did you know Philip?"

"I saw him around. We worked on different projects most of the time. He spent a lot of time away. But when I saw him lately he seemed distracted."

"How do you mean, distracted?"

Lisa shrugged. "Like he had something on his mind. I also heard him arguing with Marcus once."

"Marcus, the boss?"

"Yes."

"Did you know what it was about?"

Lisa shook her head. "No, I was waiting outside and I could hear raised voices inside Marcus's room. Then Philip came out, his face flushed. He slammed the door shut and stormed out."

"What was Marcus like afterwards?"

"Cool as a cucumber. It didn't seem to bother him."

"Did you know that Philip left for Barnham?"

Lisa nodded. "Yes, he said he was going. That was right after he had the argument with Marcus."

"I see." Dan said after a pause, "Did you know that he got a one-way ticket to Barnham? It's on his credit card bill."

"No, I didn't know that. I wonder why?"

"Me too."

"It's like he wasn't planning on coming back."

Dan nodded. "Would you say Marcus and Philip were not the best of colleagues?"

"Yes, based on what I saw. You know," Lisa leaned closer, "it's not the first time that Marcus has ruffled someone's feathers."

"What do you mean?"

"He's a bully. He likes to push people around till he gets what he wants. You know he's ex-army, don't you?"

This was news to Dan. He thought of the gravelly voice and the haughty manner. It wouldn't surprise him. Probably an officer, not an NCO like himself. "I didn't know that," he said.

"He was on track to become a one-star general, apparently. But they took him off it. Some corruption scandal about preferential treatment of a defense contractor. Marcus used to be a director on the board of that company."

Dan sat back. "Interesting."

"He left the army and set up this company. Some say he still uses his old contacts to get business."

"So, what do you do for them?"

"I look after the amplifiers in the optical fibers that form the cables. They increase the data signal as light is passed through the fibers."

"You lost me."

Lisa smiled. "Sorry to get technical, but you asked. Basically, my job is to help design the connectors in the cables. Make sure the signal is loud and strong when they get to the other end."

"That's better. So what did Philip do?"

"He was in overall charge of the network. What distance the lines would cover, how much data they could hold, over what sort of geography, stuff like that."

Dan ran his finger across his lower lip, rubbing it slowly. "He was like the designer of the network?"

"Uh-huh, you could say that."

Dan thought of the books in Philip's study. The laptop that had clearly been removed—and not by the cops. The folders on Marcus's desk. Something was rotten here and it was Synchrony Communications that smelt the worst.

"You like your job?," he asked Lisa.

"It pays the bills."

"Must be more than that. It sounds technical. Did you go to school for it?"

She nodded. "Yes, I majored in solid state technology at Atlanta Clarke, then followed it up with a masters at GSU."

Dan was impressed.

"You got brains," Dan said. And looks to match, he thought silently. "Local girl, then? Grew up around here? You don't have an accent though."

She shook her head. "I grew up in Chicago. Went to high school there. My dad was an engineer as well. He worked for an electric company, making pylons. My mom was a home-maker. Guess I always wanted to follow in my dad's footsteps."

"Makes sense," Dan said. "Listen, you know of a place to stay around here?"

"In Atlanta? Yeah, heaps. What sort of place did you have in mind?"

He couldn't go back to sleep at the house in Virginia Highlands. Just pick up his stuff, then find a safer place.

"Somewhere cheap. A midtown hotel would do. I need to stay a couple of nights, then I'll head out to Barnham."

Lisa thought for a while. "Let me ask around. A couple of my friends have apartments where they have spare rooms. They might want a lodger."

"That would be cool," Dan said. "Listen, I need to ask you something. Your office has a basement floor. Guess you knew that."

"Yes."

"They have a room there with piles of computer screens. Hand vein locks and retinal scanners. That seems pretty secure to me."

Lisa raised her eyebrows. "You went for a stroll?"

Dan shrugged.

"That room is guarded like Fort Knox," Lisa said. "They have their own secure internet server that allows access only to needed sites. All other sites are blocked."

"Like an internal network," Dan said.

"Yes, and none of the workers in there are allowed in with their phones. They have to hand them in before they start."

"How do you know this?"

"Philip used to work in there. He told me."

"What are they doing in there?"

"That's the bit he wouldn't talk about."

Lisa checked her watch and stood up. "I better head back. What will you do?"

Dan took his time before replying.

"I need to do some digging on this Marcus guy and go see Philip's daughter as well. She's a student at Emory. I might need your help with finding out about Marcus."

Lisa said, "No problem. There's something weird about this and I figure Marcus knows more. Let me know how I can help."

"Sure thing."

Dan paid the bill, said good bye to Lisa and called a cab on his phone.

CHAPTER 17

Fort Gordon
Georgia
780th Military Intelligence Brigade

Susan Gardner, MASINT (Measurement and Signature Intelligence) specialist, hunched over the two large computer screens in front of her and frowned.

She clicked on the keyboard and brought up several images, extracted data from them and superimposed them on each other. Susan's work, like that of many others in the 780th MIB, was to monitor internet signals flowing in and out of continental USA. She found cyber threats, and dealt with them. Another group in her brigade was responsible for launching cyber attacks on the hackers around the world that threatened US military installations.

Susan opened up MS Excel and used it to form a spreadsheet chart of the data she had found. Most times, she did not need fancy computer programs. She stared at the chart in front of her and her frown deepened.

Susan printed off the charts and got up from her desk. She walked across the darkened office, with analysts poring over computer screens all around her.

She knocked on the door of her Commanding Officer, Major Becker. A male voice told her to enter. Major Becker was alone. Susan brushed back some strands of her brown hair and straightened herself as she entered. She was dressed in office garb, navy blue skirt suit and black tights. Her brown hair was tied back in a ponytail. She put the spreadsheets in front of her boss. Becker looked at them.

"What is this?" he asked.

Susan said, "Sir, these are charts of signal latency in our network servers."

"All networks have slowdowns, Sargent Gardner. You know that."

"Yes sir. But these all occur at certain times of the day. Early in the morning and midday. Apart from the timings, there are other similarities. They last for the same lengths of time. I looked into several – their amplitudes are identical."

Becker raised his eyebrows. "What are you saying?"

"That there is a pattern here, sir. There is no smoke without fire, and I believe these signal slowdowns are not a fault of the servers."

"You think so?" Becker was frowning.

"So I looked around."

"Did you? Anything interesting?"

"Several things, sir. As you know, the Democrat convention's emails have been hacked. Some senators' emails, from both sides, have been leaked out. No one actually knows if the senators in question even had these emails. But the leaks show the same IP address as the senators' website."

"That could be a result of a hacking attack. The emails might not exist at all. Hackers copied them and sent it from that IP address."

"Exactly. So I looked at the signals in the convention servers, and also the senators offices. They had similar delays, at the same time of the day as us. Same amplitude. Has to be the same hacker that is causing them."

Becker said, "Carry on."

Susan was warming up. She cleared her throat. "At the time of these slowdown's sir, the networks were flooded with millions of emails."

"What do you mean? All networks have millions of emails."

"Not several million concentrated in ten minute packets, they don't. These emails were all junk and spammers. They flooded the networks with bogus traffic."

Light was beginning to dawn in Becker's eyes. "I see. A DDOS."

"That's right, sir. A distributed denial of service. Favorite ploy of hackers and spammers."

Becker leaned forward and put his elbows on the desk. "Sit down Sargent."

"Thank you, sir." Susan smoothed her skirt and sat down opposite her boss.

"What else have you found?"

"You know there was an internet outage in parts of New York and New Jersey?"

Becker said, "Near Bellport and the coast of NJ?"

"Yes. I looked into those outages as well. Similar story. Before the outages happened, they had similar signal delays. But these delays became progressively longer, till there was no transmission at all. The outage lasted for ten hours before it was fixed."

"So why doesn't it happen to us? The outage, I mean."

"Because of our dedicated dual servers. They are different from civilian ones. If one of our server's go down, another takes over. Plus, our cables are different too. Civilian cables are easier to disrupt."

"But our infrastructure can go down, and then we have an outage of our own."

Susan was silent. Becker said, "Who else have you told about this?"

"You are the first to know, sir."

Becker tapped his lips for a while, staring at the ceiling. Then he passed a hand over his head.

"You sure about the validity of the MASINT?" Becker asked.

"Yes sir. 110%"

Becker reached for the red phone on his desk. "Get me Lt. Colonel Stanley, Deputy Director of the DIA," he said.

*****

Joint Base Anacostia Bollings
Washington DC
HQ, Defense Intelligence Agency (DIA)

Lt. Colonel Chuck Stanley looked at the three men and one woman inside his office. He knew all of them, including Major Becker of the 780th MIB. The woman, Sargent Gardner, he had not seen before. And she was the one doing all the talking.

Stanley said "So what are you trying to say, Becker? That what happened in New Jersey and down in Georgia are related?"

Much to Stanley's irritation, Becker deferred to the woman again. Stanley preferred to speak to the ranking officer.

Susan said, "Sir, this was done by a machine. The software that did it has to be the same. Our coders can verify that."

Stanley said, "So where the hell is this machine, Sargent?"

"That's what we need to find out, sir. Someone is operating this machine, and this person is the hacker. So we really need to find both man and machine."

Stanley sighed. "So you are here to tell me you have no idea of the source of the problem?"

Becker took over. "Neither HUMINT or MASINT have come up with anything so far. If it is a machine, then it is unlike anything we have encountered so far. And that research has been done in collaboration with your guys here, sir."

Stanley said, "By machine you mean a computer. How can it be so hard to find a computer? Find the same IP address. It might be hidden or encrypted, well, just break the code."

Susan said, "It's actually not that simple sir. A microchip could code for this software and the chip could be hidden anywhere capable of transmitting the program. It could be in a satellite for all we know."

Chuck Stanley looked at the woman briefly. Pretty, and a nice dress. But her words hit home. She made sense, and she did not seem fazed by his presence. Most of his men found him intimidating, but not Susan Gardner. Stanley was developing a grudging respect for her.

He said, "So we are sure that these…incidents, are linked?"

Both Becker and Susan nodded. Susan said, "Yes, sir."

Stanley looked to his left, at his Sargent in Command. "Joel, call a conference of our analysts." Joel saluted and got up to leave.

Stanley called him back. "And Joel, get the Secretary of Defense as well. Tell him it's me."

CHAPTER 18

Dan got off at Emory's main campus in Druid Hill. The sprawling university occupied hundreds of acres. He had Tanya's cell number, and he had called her twice but the line was engaged once and the phone was off the second time.

The buildings were a combination of classical and modern, and were very well maintained. There was a complex of restaurants and a large public arts theatre. Young people strolled around, as carefree as one could be in a school that cost sixty thousand dollars a year to attend, and admitted just above a quarter of those who applied.

He asked in the main office for Tanya's halls of residence. He had the address from Jody already. As he walked down, he thought about what he was going to say. Hey, I'm a stranger who met your mom at the airport. By the way, your dad's gone missing, your mom is literally having a fit, and I came down here to look for him. He sighed. Maybe this was a bad idea.

He got to the college dormitory and stood outside, watching a gaggle of girls stream out the door, followed by two football jocks. Jocks looked the same the world over. Beefy, broad and permanently vacant eyes. They smiled at Dan, who didn't smile back.

He went in through the door and looked for Room 215. Second floor. He took the stairs to the landing and waited again for some students to come out of the double doors. They stood there talking, books in hand, hands gesticulating, holding up the hallway. What was it with students? They had too much time on their hands. Or was he just an old grump bag?

Dan suddenly realized how odd he must look. He was clearly not a freshman, way beyond a sophomore, more than a senior... maybe he looked someone's dad. The thought was mortifying. He ducked his head and walked into the hallway. Loud music came from one of the rooms. Rap. Jah Rule bleating about how big he was. He got to the door of 215 and knocked. There was no answer. He put one ear against the wood. Apart from the dull thud of the rap music, he couldn't hear anything. The room was empty. He should have rung. He knocked again.

"Can I help you?" a female voice asked from behind him.

Dan turned around. An interesting sight.

Three young women faced him. They wore mini-skirts and tops that finished below the breasts, showing their toned midriff and abdomen. All three had long legs, and he couldn't help but move his eyes vertically once. Perfect. Long legs and great figures. All three were smoking hot. The middle one was blonde with "Dooley's" written in red on her white top and cheerleader written all over her face. The other two were shorter, with darker hair, and just as hot. All three must be cheerleaders, Dan guessed. Tanya was a bookworm, Jody had informed him. Dan took that to mean a nerd. Well, to get in here on a scholarship one had to be a nerd. He wondered what the cheerleaders wanted from Tanya.

He cleared his throat and tried to look nonchalant. He was the older— much older, guy here.

"I am looking for Tanya Longworth. Is she here?"

The two girls at the side exchanged glances, but the one in the middle was frowning at him. The tall, really hot one. She stepped forward, her eyes narrowed.

"I am Tanya," she said. "Who are you?"

Dan stared back at the three women in front of him. When he looked closer at the blonde girl, he saw dark blue eyes that reminded him of Jody. He swallowed.

"My name is Dan. Dan Roy. I am a friend of your father's."

Tanya's eyes were suspicious. "I didn't know you were dad's friend. And why are you here?"

Her face cleared suddenly. "Is dad ok?"

Dan looked at the room. "Can we talk inside please, Tanya?"

Tanya thought for a while, then exchanged a glance with her friends. "Give me a second," she told Dan. The three women went a few paces out and talked in whispers. Dan didn't blame them. He was a total stranger. But there was no other way. From what he had seen so far, the guys out to hurt Jody meant business. Tanya was in danger, and she needed to know that.

After a while, the women came back. Dan noticed all three of them look him up and down. He was thirty-five and these girls were what, twenty years old?

He felt the heat rise to his face. He looked down and put a finger inside his collar. He scratched his head.

This was absurd. Dan cleared his throat and folded his thick arms across his chest.

Tanya said, "Alright. Come inside and tell me quickly what you have to say. My friends will stand outside. If I'm not out in five minutes they'll call security."

Dan followed Tanya inside. It was a typical college dorm room. Two beds lay on either end of the large room, with desks by their side. Bookshelves lined the wall space above the beds and the desks. A poster of Leonardo di Caprio looked down at him, smiling. Tanya flounced on the bed, and her skirt rode up dangerously high. She patted it down and folded her long legs. Dan breathed out and looked away.

In a guarded voice, Tanya said, "So what did you want to say?"

Dan told her about meeting Jody, and what happened after. He left nothing out. Tanya listened, open mouthed, shock and disbelief battling for place on her face.

She spoke immediately when Dan stopped. "What's happened to Daddy? Is he alright?" The concern in her voice was palpable.

Dan tried his best to look supportive. "I'm sure he is. Don't worry. But he went somewhere with work, and he hasn't come back as yet." He put his hands up. "But he will be back soon, I bet you."

"How do you know that? And who the hell are these people following my mom around?" Tanya was standing up straight, and looking at him sharply.

"I don't know, Tanya. But I'm trying to find out."

Tanya was breathing heavily. "And who the hell are you?"

Dan could feel the situation slipping out of control. He pulled out his cell phone. He dialed Jody's number and gave Tanya the phone. "Here, this is your mom. Speak to her. It's ringing."

Jody looked at the screen, then pressed the phone to her ear. Dan hoped and prayed Jody would answer.

"Hello, mom?" Tanya said. Dan felt relief course through him. Tanya listened intently as her mother spoke. Several times, Tanya lifted her eyes to look at Dan. Each time, Dan lowered his eyes.

Finally, Tanya hung up. She gave the phone back to Dan. Her face was more controlled. She brushed her hair back with her hands. "Thank you."

Dan said, "It's nothing, honestly. I'm in this now, too. The cops suspect me. The men who came to get your mother are now after me."

"So what do we do?"

"Tanya, listen to me. I want you to think very carefully. Do you remember seeing anything unusual in the weeks before? Was your dad acting weird? Anything you can remember would be useful."

After a while, she nodded to herself. "There was, in fact. One evening, I saw him walk to the end of our street. I was in his study, printing something. He got into a car and drove off with a couple of guys I've never seen before."

"Can you remember the car? Color, registration, make anything."

"Yeah, I do. The car was blue and it looked like a Chrysler. It was weird, because he's never done it before."

Dan felt a hammering inside his head, like someone was hitting the sides of his skull nonstop. There was a tightness in his neck and an ache behind his eyes.

"You sure it was a blue Chrysler?"

"Yes, positive."

"Anything else?"

"A man came to see him one evening. It was Friday. I had come home to pick up a dress—I had a sorority dinner that night. I opened the door to this man. He said he wanted to speak to Daddy."

"What did he look like?"

"Shorter than average, but chunky. You know, fat. He had a round face and he wore a black suit, I think. He even told me his name, when I asked him. Damn if I can remember it now."

The throbbing inside Dan's head was getting worse. "Marcus. Marcus Schopp? Is that what he said his name was?"

"Yes, that's right. How did you know?"

"He's your dad's boss. Was your mother in when these things happened? She never told me anything."

"Yes, she was. But maybe she didn't notice."

Tanya sat down again and held her head. "I can't believe this is happening."

Something in her tone bothered Dan. "Tanya?" he asked gently.

She spoke in a low voice. "I have never seen you before. But what the hell. You might as well know. Mom and Daddy don't get along anymore. They try to keep up appearances in front of me, but I know. I know."

Dan said, "It's alright."

"No, it's not. They've been drifting apart for years, really. They just act in front of me. Dad sleeps in the couch when he comes back late. I used to find him in the mornings. But it meant a lot to both of them that I came to this school. Daddy started working harder. I think that drove them apart." She picked at an invisible thread in the bed linen.

Dan came off his chair and knelt on the floor in order to face her. "You are right, Tanya. We are strangers. I know nothing about you. But let me tell you something. You coming here had nothing to do with your parents having trouble. Do you hear me? Absolutely nothing. Your parents are proud of who you are. Of who you have become."

"Yeah? Then why has Daddy disappeared?"

She was gazing at him and he saw the sadness build up until it broke over the wall and crashed out of her eyes. She put her hands on her face and sobbed. Dan felt awkward. He wanted to comfort her, but it didn't feel right. He sat there, staring at the floor.

Tanya got up and went to the bathroom. He heard her blow her nose and she came out with a tissue, drying her eyes.

"God, I'm sorry, Dan." She looked embarrassed.

Dan let out a big sigh. "Don't be. It's my fault. I should have warned you. Your mom didn't want you to know. But I had to know if you could shed any light on the matter. As it is, you've helped plenty."

"What do you mean?"

"What you told me so far. I need to look into it." He paused for a second. "Just one thing. When Marcus came around, did you hear any of their conversation?"

"No, they went into the living room and shut the door." She was standing near the window, looking out at the sunshine streaming through the trees. "Dad called me, you know."

"Really?" Dan stood up. "Since he disappeared?"

"Last week." She frowned, trying to think. "No, week before. Ten days ago."

"What did he say?"

"It was weird. He said he loved me, and everything would be alright. He told me not to speak to anyone, and not to tell anyone he called."

"Did he say where he was?" Tanya shook her head.

"Okay, Tanya, I want you to think about this. Could you hear any background sounds? Anything particular?"

Tanya was quiet for a while. "Yes, it was windy, I could hear it between his words. And a high-pitched sound, like a horse."

"A horse?"

Tanya shrugged. "Sounded like that. Who knows what it was."

"What number did her call from?"

"His own cell."

Dan thought for a while. Every cell phone call was recorded. Philip would have known that, and the fact that he could be traced from that call. Yet, he had taken that risk, maybe because he wanted to hear his daughter's voice.

Why? Was it for the last time?

"And he didn't leave any messages?"

"No."

Tanya turned around to face Dan. "Can you find my father?"

All of a sudden, she seemed like a lost girl, eyes streaked with tears, asking for help.

Dan felt a tightness in his limbs, and the slow spread of an anger that burned across his chest. He flexed his jaws before he spoke.

"I'll find him. I promise."

CHAPTER 19

"Captain!"

Mikhail Shevchenko turned at the voice behind him. He had his laptop open and was reading one of the emails sent from Kremlin. He shut the page and closed the laptop.

"Yes, Sasha."

Sasha looked excited. "The *Guboki* has returned. It's in the dock now."

"Very well, I am coming."

Shevchenko walked sedately down the gangplank as Sasha scurried ahead of him. As Shevchenko descended the stairs and entered the vast room, he heard the high whine of the crane and felt the tremor of the floor as it slid back in its semi-circle. He stood near the doorway and observed quietly. The glistening hull of the *Guboki* was resting on its holds. The crane straps were still fastened. There was a loud thud as the remainder of the floor locked into place. The number of men on the floor increased, mostly congregating around the machine.

Shevchenko strode over. Near the head of the machine, he peered closely at the removable data storage module. He gestured to Sasha, who came over and barked some orders. A man at the console chamber at the back punched some orders into a keyboard, and the clasps that hooked on the RDSM sprung free with a click. Shevchenko picked it up, and took the module out of its waterproof box. He headed towards the bridge.

"Come with me, Sasha," he ordered. The boy needed to learn.

They went up to the scientists' room next to the bridge. The two P's, they called them. Pavel and Pushkin. They took the RDSM from Shevchenko and plugged it into their system. The data was varied. It included atmospheric pressure, chemical samples and digital photographs. Most of it was technical, but the photographs and videos were what Shevchenko was most interested in.

After some time, Pushkin bought up one of the images on the large screen. The pictures were dark, but as Pushkin went through the series, they became clearer. The *Guboki* had gotten closer to the ocean bed, its flashlight reflecting off the sand. Images of a long black line emerged on the seabed, stretching out into the murky distance.

"It's there," Sasha said.

"Yes," Shevchenko murmured. "But we expected that." He watched some more, chin in his hand. "Switch to video mode and keep it on a slow frame." After a while, Shevchenko looked at his protégé.

"This stretch looks alright as well. The *Guboki* needs a rest. Can the *Krasnaya* go down later tonight?"

Sasha nodded. "Of course, Captain. I will see to it at once."

"Do not send it down without me being there, Sasha. I want to check the RDSM first."

"No problem, Captain." Sasha said. "By the way, the sonar technician wants to see you."

Together, they went to the big white golf ball on the aft deck. The sonar guys had an office next to it. The senior technician was a man called Yuri. Shevchenko patted him on the back. Yuri took his headphones off. He pointed to a screen where a graph was continuously plotting out the sound waves coming from under the ocean.

"Small sounds coming from two hundred miles away, Sir. Not whales or other big fish. Too small to be a submarine. Don't know what they are."

Shevchenko peered closely. "Keep monitoring this. Can you keep a copy of the charts and see if there is a pattern?"

"No problem, Captain."

Shevchenko's phone rang. He took his cell out and looked at the screen. He excused himself and went down the ladder into the bowels of the *Nimika*. Within five minutes he was in his room with the door shut securely. As was the usual practice, the phone rang again. He answered it this time. Both of them waited for a second as the click of the encryption came on.

"Hello, it's me," the voice said. It was Val Ivanov.

"Yes, comrade. Have you got the information?"

There was a pause. "No, but it should not be long. We have one lead that we are pursuing actively. How are you doing?"

Shevchenko sighed. The longer he stayed out here in the middle of the Atlantic the greater the chances of him being spotted. He probably had been already. His voice became impatient.

"We are going ahead as planned. But as you know, this is the secondary role of the mission. We still await the important co-ordinates."

"And they will come, I promise you. Continue to show us what you can do. There is no indication the Americans suspect anything. Not as yet. Even when they do, it will take them a few days to get to you. Do not worry. You will be warned in advance."

"Please remember what I carry. My ship contains two of the most advanced machines in the entire Russian Navy."

"I know that. That is why you were chosen for this mission, Captain. For your experience with them. Now that you are here, let us make the mission successful."

"We need to hurry up."

"Do not worry."

"Listen to me. Our propellers and engine make a huge amount of noise. Any passing submarine will pick us up on their passive sonar easily. We can always pretend we are doing research and nothing else. After all, we are more than two hundred miles away from US shores. However, we do not want the attention. I do not have to tell you the catastrophe that will begin, if these machines fall into American hands."

There was a pause at the other end. Shevchenko knew Val was digesting it slowly, and wondering if there was a threat in what Shevchenko had said. There was, he had meant it, but he wasn't afraid. Shevchenko had powerful friends in Kremlin. He wouldn't be pushed by some criminal, however powerful *he* was.

"You don't have to remind me, Captain," Val said in a soft voice.

"Good." Shevchenko hung up.

He returned to the bridge. Sasha was waiting for him.

"The *Krasnaya* is ready for departure, Captain."

"Very good. Let us go." They went down to the dry dock and checked what was needed. When Shevchenko was up with the scientists, he had his laptop with him. He opened his emails and peered at the one he wanted.

"What depth and speed, Captain?"

"Same depth and speed as the previous dive. But this time we need to do this as well."

He pointed at his laptop. Sasha and the scientists leaned closer.

"Very good, Captain," said Pushkin with a smile.

*****

Val stared at the cell phone in his hand. He was forced into being nice to Shevchenko, and he hated it. He should be threatening the old man, telling him to shut up and do his job. But Shevchenko did have a point. They needed the information as soon as possible. Sooner or later, the US Navy would realize what the *Nimika* was up to. They didn't have much time. The phone beeped.

"It's me," Val said shortly.

"Any news of him?" Direct and to the point as usual.

"No, still looking." The voice at the other end made an impatient clucking sound.

"He's hiding somewhere in Barnham."

Val was starting to get the same impression. They had looked in Atlanta and in the counties around. Neither the Mexicans nor his men had found any trace of Longworth. The man was obviously using the cash he had stolen from Val. He wasn't calling on his cell, and probably using a fake name. He could be anywhere. But yes, it made sense he was in Barnham.

"There are still a few places around here where we have eyes," Val said. "Then we can head down to Barnham."

"You need to keep this as a priority."

"It *is* a priority." Val didn't like being told what to do.

"He was delivered to you, and you let him get away. Now this other guy has joined the search."

Val grimaced. He resented the tone, but he also knew about the new guy.

The one who had smoked four Mexicans inside the house. Without using a gun. The man did sound interesting. Val wanted to meet the guy—and kill him slowly.

"Don't worry about either of them," Val growled. "Neither will be alive for much longer."

CHAPTER 20

Dan decided to take a bus back to Morningside. There was a stop on Virginia Highlands and he could walk from there. He sat by the window and stared out as the ornate buildings of the campus flashed by.

Number one. Philip had been in that blue Chrysler. With the Latino gang-bangers. What was he doing? Regardless of the answer, it was bad news. He thought of the men who had come to the house. They were now in the morgue. He needed to stop by and see Detective Brown. Find out where the ganglands were in Atlanta. Andy might have new evidence from the house, too.

Number two. Marcus Schopp. Who the hell was he? Sounded like he had a dark past. And he came around to Philip's house. Must have been something urgent. They had a shouting match in the office as well.

Number three. The tall, blond guy.

Too many questions, not enough answers. He got off the bus and jogged the last twenty minutes to the house. He hadn't run for the last week, and he was used to running five miles a day. He got to Virginia Highland covered in sweat. A short run, no more than two miles, but he felt better. There was white tape around the outside of the house.

Philip and Jody's American Dream. They had woken up one morning and the dream wasn't there anymore. He picked his way past the white tape and unlocked the front door. Not much had been cleaned up. The bodies in the kitchen had gone, leaving a stale smell of sweat behind. His black bag was still in the cupboard under the staircase. He walked through the kitchen area. There was a door leading out to the garage. He opened it and turned the light on.

The garage was large enough for two cars, but there was only one. A black Lincoln town car. Looked in good shape, too. Dan ran his hand down the side, onto the hood. No dust. The fenders gleamed. He tried the front door and it opened. It smelled of the leather seats inside. He made himself comfortable in the spacious driver's seat and looked around. There was no key in the ignition. He found it inside the dashboard drawer, tucked into the corner under some CD's. The engine sprang to life. He pressed on the gas and the engine responded. The fuel tank was almost full.

He left the engine running and went to get changed. Upstairs was still the same. Clothes and torn carpet everywhere. He took out a change of clothes from his bag: a grey shirt and blue Chinos. Then he ran down and shut the engine off. He took the keys and went back upstairs. Time for a quick shower. As he rubbed himself dry, he went to the front bedroom. He saw it almost instantly.

A car that hadn't been there before. A maroon Buick salon. Two men in the front. Parked opposite the house, but both men were checking the house out.

Had they followed him? He hadn't seen anyone on the bus. He got dressed quickly and went downstairs. The hammer and knives were missing. He picked up a smaller kitchen knife and his bag. He went to the living room. He stayed away from the windows, but could see the maroon Buick clearly. It had seen better days.

Two Mexican guys in the front seat. The driver had tattoos up the side of his neck. As he watched, the car pulled out and headed down the avenue. Dan ran into the garage. He chucked the bag in the rear seat and pressed the remote for the garage door. The Lincoln leaped out into the driveway and churned up dust as it swerved onto the street.

Ahead of him, he could see the Buick at the end of the road. It indicated and turned left, heading for downtown. Dan kept four cars behind. Traffic was light. After twenty minutes driving, the Buick nosed up north. Dan recognized some of the land around, mainly because he could see the glint of sun on the Chattahoochee River in the far left. The Buick kept pushing up, and Dan saw signs for Cobb County soon. They were leaving Atlanta.

The air conditioner was on full blast. The sky was cloudier today, and judging from the black smear around the edges of the horizon, a storm was coming. He turned on the radio to a news channel.

There was a lot of noise about a senator's connection with the Russians. His email had been hacked and some of his emails were sent to The Atlanta Herald, a local newspaper. The senator had extensive contacts with Russian businessmen, arranged trips for them to come over from Moscow, and all of these businessmen had powerful contacts in Kremlin's Red Square. His opponents were calling for him to resign. The senator was denying all knowledge of these emails, and a nationwide hunt had begun for the hacker. Dan half-listened. His eyes were on the Buick four cars ahead. It stayed on the I-75, steadfastly heading northwest.

He remembered hearing something last week on the news about the Democrat convention being hacked. A national telecommunications company was in trouble, too. Bellport, a seaside town in New York state, had suffered a blackout of its internet communication. After Bellport, several counties in New York reported similar outages. Dan shook his head. Bad news got all the headlines.

As was his habit, he flicked channels for international news. If there was a terrorist attack or hostage situation he liked to know. Not that it was his concern anymore, but old habits die hard. It seemed almost weird that he wasn't operational anymore. But then again, he wanted to be free.

He rolled down the window and a blast of warm, humid air came in through the window. They passed by an airfield on the left. He didn't know the name.

Almost an hour later, he saw signs for the city of Marietta. Main city of Cobb County. The Buick rolled off a turnpike and descended into the city. A truck trundled past Dan and he kept behind it. They were at the outer limits of Marietta, and the Buick bumped along an industrial road with warehouses on both sides. Dan stayed behind the truck, the Buick one car ahead of it. Soon the Buick indicated right and turned into a warehouse. Dan drove past it, then did a hard left and pulled into the parking lot of a large building. It was a meat packing factory.

He locked the Lincoln and walked out, heading for the warehouse. The sky had darkened above and he could hear the rumble of thunder. He checked his watch. 1500 hours. He stopped at an overgrown bush before the gates of the warehouse. He could see the Buick in there, along with two other cars. All three were empty. Gang members, having a meeting. Probably some of the shot-callers. The front door was shut and he could see the steel bar outside, which could lock the door.

There was a path snaking around to the back. There was no one at the front of the warehouse courtyard to see him. He vaulted over the gates and landed on his toes. He moved quickly. He flattened himself against the corrugated iron sides of the warehouse. The place wasn't big. A fire escape led up to a door at the top. Windows too, but they were too high up to see. He tested the fire escape stairs, then stole his way up. At the landing, he paused. He put his ear to the door. Voices inside, some being raised. Muffled; they must be on the ground. Gently, he tried the door handle. It was open. A slight crack allowed him to see inside.

Six gang members were sat around a table on the ground floor. One of them wore a red bandana. All of them had their arms and necks covered in tattoos. As he watched, one of them got up, said something, and walked to the rear of the warehouse, where he opened a door. Dan shut the fire door and sprinted down the fire escape. He ran to the back and, shielding himself against the side, he looked around the corner. The man was taking a leak. The door behind him was shut. Dan took out the knife from his belt.

He crouched down low, his face almost touching the overgrown grass. Soundlessly, he traversed the distance between them. The man was just finishing. He zipped up and Dan was right behind him, his arm clamping around the man's face, jerking him back against him. The knife edge was thrust against the carotid artery in the soft part of the neck. The man grunted and went for his gun. Dan kicked with his knee, moving the hand away. He increased pressure on the knife.

"Move again, asshole, and this knife is going all the way in," he whispered. The man went still. "Do you understand?" The man mumbled something and nodded.

"Throw your gun on the floor. Do it! Slowly!" Dan pushed the knife in. A trickle of blood wound its way down the man's neck. Dan watched as the man fumbled in his belt, took out his gun and dropped it on the floor. Dan jerked the man around till he was facing the door.

"We're going in. Take it easy. Not only will I stick the knife in, but then use your body as a shield to get out, if they start shooting. Got that?" The man nodded. Sweat poured down his face, dampening Dan's hand clamped over his mouth.

"Open the door," Dan ordered.

Together, they walked in, Dan keeping a rigid clamp on the man's face. The five men around the table didn't notice at first until one of them pointed and stood up.

Dan was less than thirty feet away from the front door. He shuffled closer. He looked at the men, all of whom were now on their feet, guns drawn.

"Sit down," Dan shouted. They ignored him.

"You want him to die? He's going to die, I promise you." Dan removed his hand from the man's mouth and pulled his head back by his hair. "Tell them asshole," he whispered. The man broke into a frightened yelp of Spanish. There was shouting at the table, with hands and guns waving. Two of the guns remained calm and pointed straight at him. He kept shuffling back until he was six feet from the front door.

The man with the red bandana shouted at the rest in Spanish. Dan guessed he was the leader. The others shouted back and he pointed his gun at them and screamed. Two of them looked down. Red bandana looked towards Dan.

"If you kill him, you will die as well." His voice was calm, unhurried.

"Okay, let me kill him then." Dan put pressure on the knife and another drop of blood tricked down. The man screamed and kicked with his legs, but Dan held him firm.

"What do you want?" Red bandana said.

"Philip Longworth. Where is he?"

The man smiled. "The gringo? You are here for him?" He shook his head. "You are a fool. The gringo is dead already."

Dan ignored that. "Was he selling for you? Cocaine?"

A snarl came up on red bandana's face. "Yes, he was." He spat on the floor. "*Puta madre*. Then he vanished without paying us."

"You don't know where he is? So why do you think he's dead?"

The man smiled, a hard, cruel smile. One of the men spoke and he snapped back at him.

Dan said, "Atlanta PD, the FBI and the DEA are on this case now. If you tell me what the hell is going on, I might be able to cut you on a deal."

Another man shouted at the leader, who shouted back. For a while, they screamed at each other, waving their guns. Something was wrong here, Dan thought. This was more than gang business. The men calmed down and the leader looked at Dan again. Dan had used the time to move closer to the front door. He dragged the whimpering gang member with him. Less than four feet away now.

"How much money does Philip owe you?"

"More than fifty grand. You got that money, *cabron*?"

Jesus Christ. Philip, you asshole. What the fuck did you do?

"Who is the tall, blond guy?" Dan asked.

The leader's eyes narrowed and he didn't say anything. One of the men shouted at him again and they went off into another verbal match. Dan cleared the remaining space to the door and kicked it open. He shoved the man inside, who stumbled and sprawled on the ground. Dan shut the front door and used the bar to lock it. He sprinted towards the meat packer's factory. He could hear shouts and screams inside the warehouse.

He got into the Lincoln, fired the engine and reversed it into the road. He slammed his foot on the gas. The wheels spun and the big car plunged forward. He was hurtling past the warehouse when the gang members came running out the side. They fired at him. Dan ducked low and kept the steering steady. A bullet tore into the body work, and another two whined overhead. Then he was past the warehouse and heading for the highway.

CHAPTER 21

McBride adjusted his hat and stared at the muddy waters of the Potomac river. It was turning warm in Washington. He liked coming to this park, where he often met his contacts. It was nice to stroll around as well. He heard the laughter of children behind him. He heard footsteps too, headed his way. He knew his men were keeping watch around him. On his earphones, he had not heard a warning. Instead, he heard something else.

"Greystalk approaching, now," a voice chirped in his left ear. McBride nodded, and waited in silence.

When politicians came to ask for help from Intercept, they never gave out their true names. Neither did they send their secretary. They came in person. Part of the reason was Intercept's deep connections in Capitol Hill. The other reason was to be safe. A brief, anonymous talk with another man in a park was safer than sending an official who could be bribed later by the media.

Greystalk sat down on the bench, next to McBride. They said hello.

Greystalk said, "Secretary of Defense called a meeting. A cyber-attack is underway."

McBride listened in silence. He said, "This have anything to do with that agent we spoke of last time?"

"Yes. A lot." They talked some more.

Greystalk said, "All our internet communications rely on those undersea cables. You know that. But the ones being targeted are actually the dark ones."

McBride said, "The cables for military use."

"Yes."

"We need to know how they got the location. Supposed to be a secret."

McBride said, "There is a mole. Also, you heard the internet problems at Bellport?"

"Yes. A big line of cables land at Bellport. Right from London. One of our most important communication links to Western Europe."

They were silent for a few seconds.

McBride said, "What do you want?"

"Bring it to an end. Whatever it takes. But keep it silent. The President does not want to activate any federal units. No special forces. Delta and Navy SEAL's are out. This is a strictly deniable mission. Got that?"

"No political fall-out."

"Yes."

"Do you have anyone down there?"

McBride allowed himself a grim smile. "As a matter of fact, I think we do."

*****

Dan kept to the speed limit and drove steadily down the I-75. The first few drops of rain arrived, and thunder grumbled overhead. He kept an eye on the rearview, but there was nothing. He wasn't being followed. His cell beeped and he looked at the screen. He didn't recognize the number.

"Hello?"

"Dan, this is Lisa. Where are you?"

"Just heading back from Marietta. What's up?"

"I had a look into Marcus's old files from the DoD. They were classified, so I had to get a friend who works in DoD's Washington DC records office to release them to me."

"You didn't have to do that."

"Yes, I did. If there is something weird going on, I need to know. Marcus might go down, then the company might fold. I'm going to lose my job. This is about me as well."

"Alright. Why don't we meet up to talk about it?"

"Cool. Same café?"

In one hour, he was back in downtown Atlanta. Rain was falling in a constant drizzle now. Lightning flashed as he parked the car and walked out towards the Centennial Park. Lisa was waiting inside. She had an umbrella folded behind her seat.

"Jeez, you're wet."

Dan shrugged. "Just a little drizzle, that's all. You ordered?" He was suddenly hungry.

They got coffee and Dan ordered a turkey and cheese melt. He sipped the coffee and closed his eyes. He had needed that.

"Are you okay?" Lisa asked.

"Yes, fine. What did you find out about Marcus?"

"It's interesting. He was based in the Pentagon after he was discharged from active duty. There were no concerns while he was deployed. When he came back, he worked for some defense contractors, then applied for the Pentagon. His first job as an adjutant lieutenant colonel was to procure a license for long-range mortar shells. Well, one of the contractors he had worked for made the shells, and despite a competitive tendering process, they got it." Lisa clasped her hands together and looked thoughtful. "That's not all. This pattern repeated itself over the next two years. He was rumbled finally, and kicked out."

"Do you have the reports with you?"

"I couldn't print them out. But I have them at home on my laptop. You're welcome to have a look."

"Thanks."

"Are you still looking for a place to stay?"

Dan nodded.

"Well," she said. "If it's only for a night or two, you can rest on my couch."

Dan wiped his mouth and shook his head. "No, I don't want to inconvenience you."

"You won't be, I promise. By the way, have you seen this?" Lisa took out a folded newspaper from her bag. It was the Atlanta Herald. The front page was news of the senator who was being accused of being a Russian spy. She turned to one of middle pages and handed the paper to Dan.

It was a report on the four gang members he had killed at Philip's house. There was a photo of the exterior of the house.

"That's Philip's house, isn't it?" Lisa asked.

Dan told her what had happened. Her hand went to her neck. It stayed there, massaging nervously.

"My God. Do you think other gang members will come back?"

Dan sighed and told her about what he had just learned about Philip. She listened with wide eyes. When Dan had finished, she held her forehead. "Philip was selling drugs? Cocaine?"

Dan nodded. "And it looks like he owed them money as well."

"Why would he be selling cocaine?"

Dan shrugged. "To make money. He was in debt, and I don't think he was earning enough. It's a dumb plan, but maybe he got sucked into it and carried away."

"So now what?"

"We still have to find him. I need to see Marcus again. First off, can I come to your place and see the reports?"

It was six o'clock and Lisa had finished work. They drank their coffee and headed out to her apartment. Lisa lived north of Midtown, near the Botanical Gardens. Dan drove up through the line of red tail lights smudged in the rain-splattered windscreen. The air-con was on and the wipers worked full time. It took them almost an hour to get to Lisa's place.

It was a new apartment complex two blocks away from the gardens. It was made of white and black marble, with a garden courtyard at the front. Blue, red and yellow lights lit up the plants and trees. What the realtors liked calling a luxury development. Dan drove in and parked at the underground lot. He followed Lisa up into the apartment. The place was chic and minimal, with two bedrooms, a balcony and a bathroom.

"Have a seat," Lisa indicated the couch in the reception in front of the TV.

"Thanks," Dan said. He sat down, looking at the art work on the wall. Lisa returned with her laptop. She showed Dan the emails from her colleague at the DoD. Dan clicked on the attachments. The reports looked genuine enough. They were details of disciplinary actions against Marcus Shoppe. He had been warned not to carry out preferential canvassing for contracts, but had continued to do so. Eventually, military police had got involved, and he had been court martialed. Scant evidence was found against him, and he was let off with a light sentence.

"Very hard to prove any actual wrongdoing," Lisa said, as she watched Dan read the last report.

He nodded. "Yes. Apart from the fact that he worked for those companies. What time does Marcus leave the office?"

"About now, sometimes later."

"Do you know what car he drives?"

"A blue Toyota salon."

Dan stood up. "It's time I paid him another visit."

Lisa gave him a key for the apartment. Dan told her not to wait up for him. She showed him the smaller bedroom he would be sleeping in. It was next to hers. He thanked her and left.

CHAPTER 22

He parked in the red brick Victorian house opposite Schopp's office. He turned off the ignition and the lights and waited. The rain was letting up, and the roads were slick. Lights were still on inside, and he saw one of the guards strolling around in the courtyard. He checked his phone and gave Jody a quick call.

He needed to get Jody and Tanya out of Atlanta, but he didn't want to explain that on the phone. He spoke to Jody briefly, not divulging what he had learnt about Philip just now. He hung up and continued to wait. He turned the radio on. More on the news about the slow upload speeds that were affecting most of Georgia. Important emails were not getting sent. Computers were crashing across the state, worse in Atlanta than anywhere else. Dan turned up the news, listening.

At 8:00 p.m. all the lights in the office went off. Shortly after, a black pick-up truck left. Dan figured that contained the guards. The next car to leave was a Toyota salon. In the streetlights, he could see the dark blue color. He waited a beat, then followed.

Traffic was less now and soon they were up in leafy DeKalb Avenue. There was no car between them. Dan stayed fifty meters behind, but it was pretty obvious that the two cars were headed in the same direction. Signs for a development called Lakeside Views appeared and the Toyota turned in. Dan drove past, then pulled onto the dirt sidewalk. After ten minutes he drove back towards the development. It was a gated community. The guards at the security room flagged him down. Dan lowered his window as the guard stepped out.

"Message for Marcus Schopp. Philip Longworth has been found, and wants to speak to him urgently. Tell him it's Dan, Philip's friend."

The guard looked at Dan and the car, then went up the steps. He spoke on the phone, then came back.

"Okay, he'll see you. Its number fourteen, the third house on the left." Dan gave the guard a thumbs-up, and drove in through the open gates.

It was a detached modern villa, Spanish style. The rest of the buildings were similar. Dan ran up the steps and pressed the bell. The door opened, but it was on a chain. The round figure of Marcus Shoppe stood framed in the light.

"You alone?" Schopp drawled in his low voice.

"Yes."

Schopp peered out through the door. Then he took the chain off and opened it. Dan shut the door behind him.

"In here," Schopp said. Dan followed him into an opulent drawing room. Chandeliers hung from the ceiling. Schopp pressed a button on a remote and steel blinds came down over the windows. He turned to Dan. He was still wearing his blue work suit. His features were softer, but his eyes were wary.

"You found Philip?"

"No, I lied. I couldn't get in here otherwise."

Schopp's face swelled and turned purple. His eyes became black slits and a vein popped in his forehead. "You son of a bitch!" he screamed. He threw the remote on a sofa. "I can't believe I listened to your shit. You son of a bitch."

Dan regarded him calmly. "You need to tell me what you know about Philip, Marcus."

Schopp was staring at the floor, shaking his head. "You don't know shit. You're going to get us all killed. God damn it." He began to pace up and down the room.

"You know Philip was selling cocaine, didn't you?"

Schopp came to an abrupt halt. He stared at Dan. "You don't know anything. Nothing."

Dan stepped forward. He thought of Tanya, blaming herself for her parent's marriage and now for her father's disappearance. He thought of Jodie, sitting in that hotel room, scared and worried.

"Listen to me. I told you already, four gang-bangers came into Philip's house last night. They wanted Philip. I dealt with them. Today, I followed their friends to Marietta. I found out how much Philip owes them. He's got a daughter and wife who are also in danger."

Schopp was pacing around again. "What do you want me to do?"

"Who is the tall, blond guy?"

Schopp stopped again. There was a fear in his eyes that Dan had not seen before. He swallowed, began to say something, then walked away again.

"You had an argument with Philip in the office before he left for Barnham. Before that, you went to see him at his house. What for?"

Schopp sat down heavily on the sofa and covered his face in his hands. He mumbled something.

"Talk to me, Marcus."

Schopp turned to him and smiled. That surprised Dan. It was an ironic smile. "You call yourself a friend, and you don't know anything about Philip."

"Then tell me. His daughter and wife deserve to know."

Schopp sighed heavily. "Yes, Philip had started selling cocaine. It's not hard. There are plenty of dealers on every street corner. Mainly the Latino gangs. Plenty of demand as well. You wouldn't believe how popular that white powder is in this city. Philip had to do something. His life was spiraling out of control."

Dan waited. Schopp passed a hand over his bald head and stared down at the carpet.

"He had cancer. Of the glands, and in his blood. Lymphoma or leukemia—some shit like that. He didn't tell his family, because he didn't want them to worry. He needed money for the medical bills. Chemotherapy and shit. He couldn't get insurance. No one would give him a loan against the house. So he had to do this."

Dan felt a throbbing headache inside his skull. He closed his eyes, feeling the pressure behind them. He remembered the stacks of unpaid medical bills on the floor of Philip's study.

"Why did he tell you?"

Marcus said, "I was his only friend. He helped me set the company up after Dynamic Corp, my previous company, failed."

"What else?" Dan said.

Schopp shook his head. "Listen to me. Go back and wait for him to return. You're going to get us all killed."

"Is Philip still alive?"

"I don't know," Schopp whispered. He looked up at Dan. "I'm begging you. Leave this alone."

"What's going on, Marcus?"

"You're way in over your head in this. I'm telling you, you'll get us all killed. Now get the hell out of here."

CHAPTER 23

Lisa was in bed by the time Dan got back. He let himself in with her key. He got changed and lay down on the small bed. He had difficulty fitting into it. He gave up after a while, got up and transferred the bedding to the floor. He lay down and sighed. Much more comfortable. He thought of Philip. He wondered if Jody knew anything about his illness. Philip probably hid it all. Couldn't speak to anyone… apart from Marcus Schopp, it seemed. He saw his life slowly wither away and fade, like he was watching it from a train speeding away. Then it took a life of its own, dark and maleficent.

There was a lot Schopp was hiding. He was scared. Something bigger, much bigger than the cocaine. Maybe something related to Marcus' past. Dan thought until he couldn't think anymore, then fell asleep.

He woke up once at 5:00 a.m., then fell back asleep. Bright light spilling in through the open window woke him up again. He got up and stretched. Eight o'clock. He had slept for a good eight hours. He went out into the kitchen. There was a note on the counter.

"Off to work. Croissants out, and OJ in the fridge. Help yourself to coffee. Lisa."

Dan started by doing some yoga. He did some Pranayama to cleanse his lungs out, drawing the air in to the pits of his stomach before letting it go slowly. He flexed the small joints—wrists, elbows, ankles and then did the fourteen steps of the *karthik asana*. He was sweating by the time he finished. He showered and ate breakfast, then left.

He fired up the Lincoln and drove down to Atlanta PD. He called Andy Brown on the way in. He was at the office. Dan was shown in. Brown sat in an open cubicle, next to Harris and in a line with other detectives. A patrolman pulled someone in handcuffs and orange jail suit ahead of Dan as he walked in. Brown stood up and shook hands with Dan.

"Found anything yet?" he asked. Dan took a seat next to him.

"I was going to ask you the same question," Dan said.

"Fingerprints and DNA showed the gang members. There are other DNA samples, but nothing shows up on our databases."

"Nationally?"

"Nothing." He leaned closer to Dan and jerked a thumb. "By the way, the chief wanted to interview you. I submitted a statement on your behalf. It was an act of self-defense, and there are no relatives lining up to press charges. I took care of it."

"Thanks," Dan said. He told Brown about Philip and the cocaine, and about Marcus. Brown raised his eyebrows as he listened. Then he shook his head. "Poor bastard. You reckon this is all true?"

"The part about Philip's illness is true. I saw those unpaid medical bills myself. I could ask Carter Medical, but I know they won't give away confidential information."

"So what's left?"

"I need to head down to Barnham. See what Philip was up to there."

"You know where to go?"

Dan nodded. "Lisa will get me the address of the place. It's a small town anyway." He glanced at his watch. He said goodbye to Brown and got going.

He drove south, heading for Hartfield-Jackson Airport. Fifteen minutes of traffic later he was in Grove Park. He drove through a wide avenue with tall Project buildings on the left and dilapidated brown brick houses on the right. Clumps of young men hung around in street corners. Dan drove into a drug store parking lot and pulled up. He counted the money he had. One hundred and fifty. Should be enough for what he needed. He rang Tanya and spoke to her. She was in-between classes, and they spoke quickly.

He went into the drug store. The owner was Asian, middle-aged, spiky hair with glasses. He looked at Dan and rubbed his eyes inside his glasses. Dan slid him a five-dollar bill.

"Where's the nearest gun store?"

The man looked at the bill and smoothed it. He put it in his pocket.

"Union Street and Haven junction. Down left, five minutes' walk."

"Thanks. Can I leave my car here for ten minutes?"

The gun shop was down an alley. He looked around him, then went in. The iron grill door chimed when he opened it. A squat, fat man with large eyes stared at him.

"I need a Sig Sauer P226, suppressed. Fifteen clip magazine, and two boxes of extra rounds."

The man scratched his belly. "Let me have a look," he grumbled.

He came back in a few seconds. He put a box on the counter, opened it and picked out the grey gun. Dan took it. The familiar weight and feel in his hand was comforting. He slipped the magazine out. Empty as expected. He checked the serial number. Intact. He nodded at the man.

"What round does this take?"

"I got two Sig P226's. One chambers the 40 Smith Wesson round, and another for 357 Sig. Hang on." He walked off and came back in a minute. "I got the 9mm as well. Which one do you want?"

"You got all three?"

The man raised his eyebrows and smiled. He had two front teeth missing. "We got it all, man" he said. "Which one do you want?"

Dan thought for a while. He wanted a heavier round than the 9mm. He wanted to carry an assault rifle, but it would be much harder to disguise. "I'll go for the 357."

The man grinned at Dan again. "Heavy duty, huh?"

Dan stared at him impassively until he stopped smiling. He ducked underneath the counter and came out with two boxes. Dan checked them. 357 V crown nickel plated cartridges. Hollow tip. 20 in each box. He took four of them.

"How much?"

"One hundred twenty-five."

"I need a knife as well."

"What type?"

"A kukri."

"A what?"

A forlorn hope. "Never mind. Have you got a Force Recon commander, about 12 inches with handle?"

"Think so."

"That will do for now."

The knife was in a black nylon sheath and Dan pulled it out. The grip felt good. Not as good as his kukri, but it would more than do the job. He swung his right wrist around in circles, flashing the knife in different directions.

The shop keeper was watching him. "You a knife man, huh?"

"You could say that."

He walked back to the parking lot. A couple of kids were trying to look inside the driver's side window. Dan approached them slowly.

"Can I help you?" The kids turned around and looked at Dan, a grin on their faces. Dan stared back at them, and the grin faded. They shrugged and walked off. Dan got into his car and drove out, heading up towards Druid Hill. It was past eleven o'clock and the traffic was thickening. He got to the turn before Emory University and parked the car in a side road where he could still see the street ahead coming down the hill from the college. He put the loaded Sig in his glove box. He wound both front windows down. The folded knife was in his front belt line.

He waited. After ten minutes he saw Tanya, coming slowly down the hill. She was dressed in blue jeans and a pink half sleeve top. Dan put the windows up and took the Sig in his hand. A few moments later, he saw them.

Two men, walking faster. As they went past the side road, Dan locked the car, put the Sig in his back pocket and sprinted after them. He turned left, down the hill. Ahead of him, he could see the two men. They wore dark jeans with holes in them, and leather jackets. In front of them, he could see Tanya. There was a nature reserve at the bottom of the hill, and Tanya headed into the woods. The two men followed. Dan increased his pace. As he got into the woods, he spotted the two men in front.

They were spread apart, looking around. He couldn't see Tanya.

CHAPTER 24

Dan stepped behind a tree as one of the men turned around. He heard their footsteps moving ahead in the silence, and peered out. They were going deeper into the forest. He followed, keeping close to the trees, crouching down low so the men didn't see him. The Sig was out in his right hand. The path dipped in the middle and he saw a flash of blonde hair ahead. Tanya. The men had seen her too, and increased their pace. In the seclusion of the woods, the sound of footsteps was loud. Tanya looked back. She saw the men and broke into a run. So did the men, and behind them, Dan. Tanya was fit, and she ran fast. The men were slower. There was a stream in the way and Tanya jumped over it, but she slipped and fell on the other side.

The men splashed into the water. Tanya got up and ran again. The path curved upwards, dense green foliage on either side. It was slippery as well, and it slowed her down. She held on to a tree trunk and pulled herself up.

The men had crossed the stream when one of them caught his friend's arm and pointed back. Dan was running behind them openly now. They took their guns out. One man stayed behind while the other ran after Tanya. The one who stayed pointed his gun at Dan. Dan dropped to his knee, Sig held in both his hands.

He aimed at the midriff and squeezed off two shots just as he heard the man's non-suppressed weapon crash out a round. He had rolled over by then, and the round whizzed over his head. Dan was on the ground now, wet with mud, but ready for the kill shot. He didn't need it. His previous rounds had found their mark. The man was on the ground. His arms were twitching. Dan fired another two and the body shook, then stilled.

Dan heard a woman's scream. He got up and ran, jumping over the stream. He fell on the other side, rolled over and ran up the path. Above him, the man had almost caught up with Tanya. She was finding it hard on the slippery path. Her running trainers gave her no grip, and she was on all fours, going up slowly. The man looked behind, saw Dan, and fired. Dan fell to the ground and rolled into the bushes. The shot thundered and zipped into the bushes harmlessly, but he slipped and fell further back.

He clawed with his hands, fighting for purchase on the ground. The man was standing, realizing Dan's predicament. He was aiming his gun at him. Dan didn't have any time. He dug his trunks into the ground, slowing himself. He fired twice in quick succession. One shot up, one down. The man's head snapped back like he had been punched by a heavyweight boxer, the gun arm dropped and his legs buckled. A red mist sprayed up where his head had been.

Dan grabbed a heavy root. The slope wasn't too steep, but his weight meant he slid easily down unless he stopped himself. His feet found support in a rock and he lifted himself back up on the path. He swung the gun around. No one else following. He allowed himself a few seconds, breathing hard, staring at the stream below. Nothing. He looked up and saw Tanya's mud-stained face peeking out the bushes. He reached her, and squeezed her shoulder.

"You okay?" Dan asked her.

She nodded in silence, her face drawn and white. "You did well. Really well," Dan said.

He crouched in front of the first dead man. He had stopped a bullet with his face. Result—not much face left. Dan patted him down and found a Glock 22. He used his shirt to pick the weapon up and put it in his pocket. The man had a wallet with some bills and change. No ID. He lifted the shirt and had a look at the chest. No tattoos. Same on the hands and neck. They went down to the other man, sprawled on his back near the stream. Dan looked closely at the face. Caucasian. Swarthy, heavy built. Could be Russian or Eastern European. There was a tattoo on his left wrist. Something written in Cyrillic letters. Probably Russian.

Dan frisked him quickly. The wallet had some money again, but no driving license, credit card or social security card. He had a Glock 22 as well. Dan picked it up and checked the serial number. He put the gun in his back pocket too, again using his shirt to pick the weapon up by the butt. He picked up all the shell cases from the rounds.

They walked down towards the road. Dan glanced at Tanya. She was very quiet. Withdrawn. She could be in shock, but overall, she was taking it very well.

Tanya pushed back the hair falling on her face. She nodded. "Okay, I guess." She looked around her.

"Where to now?"

"Reckon we can go back to your dorm room to clean up?"

"I guess so."

Where the nature reserve ended and the roads began, Dan stopped and checked the street. No cars parked with a driver sitting, waiting, watching. He grabbed Tanya's hand and they walked back up the hill towards the university. They got some funny looks as they went into her dorm. Inside her room, Dan let Tanya get changed.

When she came out, she was running her hand through her long hair, head bent to one side. She asked him, "How did you know?"

"I had my doubts when they turned up at your parent's house after I left you. I figured they must have followed me. More worrying, they were keeping an eye on you. I needed to flush them out." He looked at her. "You did well," he repeated.

She sat down next to him. "What's going on, Dan?"

"I am starting to find out, I think. But it will still take time. For now, it's important that you're somewhere safe."

"If I stay on campus, I should be safe."

"Maybe, but you can't stay on campus like a hermit. Your friends might want to party in town, and you could go with them. Until this blows over, I think you should stay somewhere else."

"Like where?"

"Where your mom is right now, at the hotel."

Tanya packed the things she needed, then they headed out towards downtown. Dan drove carefully, keeping an eye out for any tails. If there was, they were damn good, because he saw nothing.

In the hotel, Jody was cautious about opening the door. Her eyes lit up when she saw her daughter. They hugged, and the tears fell spontaneously. Dan stepped inside and shut the door.

He cleared his throat. The two women looked at him. Dan said, "You need to get out of Atlanta for a while."

Jody said, "Why?"

"Because it's not safe. There are gangs everywhere in this city, and I have a feeling we are looking at a combination of different gangs that are after you. Well, after Philip." His mind raced over, wondering if he should bring up Philip's drug dealing. Then he decided against it. Jody did not seem to know a lot about her husband's life. Even if she did know about the drugs, there wasn't a great deal she could tell Dan. But one thing was bothering him still.

"Jody, when they got into your house, they had keys. Had your or Philip's keys been stolen or lost before Philip disappeared?"

Jody thought, then shook her head. "No. I don't think so."

Tanya was silent for a while, staring down at her hands. Her eyes were clear when she looked up at Dan.

"What was Daddy mixed up in?"

"I don't know yet," he said.

"Is he dead?" Her voice was flat.

"I don't know."

She looked away and tightened her jaws. "Damn it."

Tanya said, "You can't do this on your own. You need my help."

Dan smiled. "I'll try and do as much as I can. I'll call when I need your help. Right now, I want you to be safe."

"But where?"

Dan looked at both of them and said, "I have a house in Bethesda. It's not been lived in a great deal in the last few years as I have mostly worked abroad. But you are welcome to stay there till this blows over."

Jody seemed to do a double take. "You're gonna let us stay in your house?"

"There's no one else staying there, Jody. Might as well get used. Unless you have family that you can stay with."

Jody looked at Dan and shook her head. "No, we don't."

Jody came forward. She reached out and held Dan's hand. Her touch was warm, and Dan felt a hint of embarrassment.

Jody said, "You're a kind man, Dan. You don't show your true feelings, but your actions speak louder than any words."

Dan didn't say anything. He took out his cellphone and called his realtor in Bethesda. She was still in the office. Dan explained that he wanted his house to be opened for the Longworths' and agreed on a time and place for them to meet.

Tanya helped Jody pack, and the three of them went downstairs to the parking lot.

CHAPTER 25

Val Ivanov stood by the stream in the woods and looked down at the dead body. There was another one further up the path. Val kicked the body.

"Idiot," he hissed. He could guess what had happened. Small footprints of a girl's sneakers were everywhere. They had followed the girl without checking if someone was following *them*. He walked up the slope to where the other body lay crumpled. Artin was going through his pockets.

"Wallet and gun gone," Artin said, looking up at Val. Val squatted. The man's face was non-existent. He looked around the body and further out in the grass. No shell cases. The killer was meticulous. He turned to Artin.

"How did we find them?"

"Two *Bratok* came to look for them. They were late for the evening hand-over. Took them a while to find the bodies."

"What about the girl?"

"We sent a man inside, dressed like a college kid. She's not in her dorm."

"Now she's missing too?"

Artin stood up slowly and backed away. "We will keep looking…"

"Shut up!" Val turned and stormed down the path. The three men at the bottom scattered. Val clamped down on his jaws. Goddamn it. The girl had a protector, and he knew who it was. That man who came to look for Philip. Dan Roy. He had wasted the Mexicans, and now his own *Bratok*. It was time he paid the price. Val turned to Artin.

"That big bastard who's been hanging around Longworth's house. It's time we had a meeting."

*****

Dan drove Tanya and Jody down to Hartfield-Jackson and dropped them off at the boarding gates. Dan felt embarrassed when Tanya hugged him. He let go quickly, turned around and left. They had the keys to his house, and from

Dulles Airport would take the train to Bethesda. Dan felt relieved that they were out of harm's way. He could now concentrate on the job at hand.

Dan was walking back to the short stay parking lot when his cell buzzed. Caller ID hidden. He answered.

"It's me, Brown."

"What's the matter?"

"Where are you?"

"Heading back uptown."

"I need to tell you something." Dan didn't like the tone of Brown's voice. He waited.

"Marcus Schopp is dead. A patrolman found his body inside a car registered to him. Two shots to the head, close range."

Dan felt a cold numbness spreading into his limbs. He leaned against a concrete post in the parking lot.

"Where and when?"

"On a quiet street, mid-town. Found this morning around 8:00 a.m. Dead for an hour, at least. His cell phone and wallet were gone. Keys were in the ignition."

Dan thought quickly. "Any damage to the car?"

"No."

"Any sign of struggle?"

"No."

"Forensics?"

"Nada. Going through it now, but nothing exciting. I'll keep you in the loop, if something turns up."

"Thanks for letting me know."

"You went to see him last night, didn't you?"

There was no point in denying it. The security had seen him, and he might have been spotted by the neighbors as well.

"Yes, I did."

Brown sighed. "Look, I gotta call you in. Just give me a statement. Keep the captain happy. No one's pressing charges."

"Do you want me to come now?"

"Yes. And Dan?"

"Yeah?"

"Be careful, buddy." Brown hung up.

Dan got to the Lincoln and sat, clutching the steering wheel as he thought to himself. He needed to get in touch with Lisa. Make sure she was okay.

"Hello?" It was a relief to hear her voice. She sounded loud.

"Marcus Schopp is dead."

"I heard. I was just about to call you." Her voice was strident, anxious.

"Are you okay?" Dan said.

"No, I'm not. What the hell is going on, Dan? You went to see the guy last night and this morning he's wound up dead." She stopped. "Sorry, I know how that sounded. I didn't mean it like that. I'm worried, Dan. Just really worried. About you, more than anything else. I don't know what to do." The high pitch had come back in her voice. She was losing it, he could tell. He gripped the phone harder.

"Hey, calm down. I'm fine. Just take it easy. Where are you?"

"At the office."

"Why don't I meet you for a coffee? At the usual place?"

Lisa agreed. Dan hung up.

As he sat stewing in the traffic and ruminating over the day's events, he noticed the car. A red Ford, about four cars behind on the second lane. The driver was a woman, and she had a passenger in the back. He had seen the car as he had come out of the parking lot at the airport. As they nudged up slowly on the black asphalt river of motors and humanity, Dan changed lanes. The car stayed in the same lane. Past downtown, the traffic was less, and he speeded up. The Ford accelerated and stayed four cars behind. Dan took the turnpike to get on the road for Lisa's apartment. The car followed. As he went into Lisa's road, the car drove past, speeding around the bend.

Dan went into Lisa's apartment and got changed. Then he drove back downtown. The rain had relented and the humidity was less. Dark clouds still scudded low across the sky. That didn't stop the heat, however. It was still hot. Maybe not in the nineties, but still high eighties, he reckoned. Lisa was sitting at an outside table, waiting for him. She waved at him.

Dan slid into a seat and gazed at her. "Are you alright?"

She looked down and picked her nails. "Sorry about earlier."

"No problem. I know this is weird."

"I feel bad. I checked the guy out, thought he was up to something. Now he winds up dead."

"Lisa, he *was* up to something. So was Philip. Marcus was running scared. I reckon Philip is, too. If he's still alive."

"You think he is?"

"Yes, I think so. If he was dead they would have found him by now." He shrugged. "Or maybe they just haven't found his body as yet. Look, all I know is that I need to keep looking."

The waitress came and they ordered coffees. As Lisa sipped hers she said, "Let's head back to my apartment after this."

Dan shook his head. "I have to go to the police station." Dan told her about his conversation with Brown.

"Jeez, Dan. This keeps getting worse."

"You aren't going back to work?" Dan asked.

"I don't have to. I've taken the rest of the week off."

"I reckon that's good for you. Get a break, while things cool down."

"It's not just that. I don't even know if the company will remain open now that Marcus is dead."

Dan leaned forward. "Hey, I'm sure it will. Don't worry."

They finished their coffees and left. As they drove, Dan glanced at her.

"Do you mind if I stay one more night at yours?"

Her face was impassive. "Sure, no problem."

"But tomorrow morning I'll be gone."

"Gone where?"

"I need to head down to Barnham, where Philip was last seen."

Lisa stared out the window at the traffic. "I'm coming with you."

"No, Lisa. I'll be looking around, asking questions. If Philip is hurt, then the men responsible will come after me. I can't have you around there as well."

"I can look after myself."

"I know you can," he said gently. "This is not about that. If something happened to you, I wouldn't forgive myself."

"I *said* I can handle myself, Dan. Look, I have three days' leave. I can sit at home and worry about what you're doing, or I can come and sit by the seaside, catch some rays. You know what I'm saying?"

Dan sighed. "You aren't going to listen to me, are you?"

She grinned for the first time. "Hell no."

*****

Dan drove down to the police station and presented himself to the desk. In an interview room Andy Brown stood up and shook hands. There was a woman Dan hadn't seen before. She wore blue pants and a blue jacket. She showed Dan her badge.

"Captain Andrea Hodge," the woman said in a flat voice. Hodge had a sharp beak of a nose and flat, black eyes that went with her voice. Her hair was raven black too, her skin tanned. Dan stared at her briefly, then at Brown. Dan was getting a bad feeling.

"Sit down," Hodge said. "Can you say your name for the recorder?"

"Am I under arrest?"

"No, you are not," Hodge said. "But we need to ask you questions."

Dan looked at them in turn. Brown shrugged, trying to put Dan at ease.

"Where were you the morning Marcus Schopp was murdered?"

"Sleeping."

Hodge gave Dan a cold look. "Don't get funny on me, Mr. Roy. There's been a murder and you are a suspect."

"I was sleeping at a friend's house in Atlanta."

"Can this friend vouch for you?"

"She can, yes."

Hodge wrote something down and nodded. "Why did you go to see the deceased the night before?"

"I'm here to look for my friend's husband, who is missing. He worked for Marcus, hence I went to see him."

"It's a gated compound. How did you get in?"

Easy does it. "I said I had information that was important to him."

"What information?"

Dan shrugged. "About Philip. He let me in."

Hodge had that dead-eyed fish stare that Dan didn't like. "Then what happened?"

"He said he couldn't help me. So I left."

"Bullshit," Hodge said. She leaned forward. "You told him you had information on Philip so he let you in. What information?"

"He was in financial difficulty. Bills and college fees."

"What else?"

"That's it."

Hodge sat back in her chair and glanced at Brown. He didn't say anything.

"Why are you holding back?" Hodge said softly.

Dan folded his hands across his chest. Hodge's eyes flickered over his body. "I'm not," Dan said.

"Let me tell you something, Mr. Roy. I got a call from the FBI today. They want to know what happened to Marcus Schopp. Do you know why the FBI is interested?"

Dan shook his head. "No."

"The FBI got a call from the Pentagon. They would send Military Police, but Marcus was a civilian. Do you follow?"

Dan nodded. "Military Police would not investigate the death of a civilian, even if he was ex-Army."

"So why the hell is the Pentagon so interested in a cable engineer?"

"I don't know," Dan said.

Hodge flexed her jaws. Brown remained silent. "You arrive in Atlanta, and Philip Longworth's house gets trashed."

"Correction," Dan said. "I surprised them."

"Whatever. Then they come back, and you," she paused for effect. "You single-handedly blow them away. I got four dead gang members, a dead former army guy, and another guy missing. Not to mention his wife and daughter. His wife has not filed a report. Don't you find that a little odd?"

Dan didn't answer that. Brown scratched his lower lip and did his bored look.

"What I'm trying to say, Mr. Roy," Hodge said, "is that we have the FBI involved in this now. We have pressure. To find things out. And you are holding back."

Pressure. "If I knew something, I would tell you."

Hodge scraped her chair back. She flicked the digital tape recorder off. She gave Dan one last dead stare.

"Get him out of here," she told Brown.

Brown walked Dan to the door and down the steps. "Sorry about that," he said.

"Don't be. This shit's gone far enough."

"This is something big, Dan. Really big. I don't know what exactly, but the FBI is pretty pissed. Apparently, this guy Marcus was someone important. I don't know why. The Feds are being the Feds, keeping their cards close to their chests. There *is* something the Captain doesn't know yet."

"Like what?"

"The fingerprints finally came up with something. We had to go global. Interpol gave us this guy. Vyalchek Ivanov. Second generation Russian immigrant. From Brighton Beach in New York. Big kahuna in the Russian organized crime ring. They call themselves the *Bratok,* or Brotherhood. Got chapters in every major American city. Drugs, prostitution, extortion, you name it. This guy's a real douche bag. There's a rumor he killed one of his own men a few weeks ago, 'cos he let someone escape. He's been in a couple of times himself, for armed robbery, then extortion."

"Who knows?"

"Harris and myself. I have to tell the captain soon. Thought you would like to know."

Dan nodded. "Thanks." He told Brown about the two men he had just killed. Brown put his hands on his hips and looked up at the sky. "Jesus Christ."

"One of them had a tattoo on his wrist. Pretty sure the writing on the tattoo was Russian."

CHAPTER 26

Dan headed back to Lisa's. He spotted the red Ford again. The driver was holding back now, staying six cars behind. Dan drove slowly, making sure he kept the car in his sights. When he pulled into Lisa's apartment complex the red Ford was gone.

Dan let himself in with the key. Lisa was sitting in the sofa, her feet up on the coffee table, her eyes on her laptop. She glanced up as Dan entered. Her hair was tied up in a ponytail, and she was wearing pink shorts that showed off her shapely legs. Dan felt his eyes travel up and down her.

"Hey," Lisa said. "How'd it go with the cops?"

Dan told her, including the part about Tanya. Lisa's eye widened.

"They attacked your cousin?"

"The Russian mob is on the case as well. It's getting serious."

"Dan, I reckon you should let the cops handle this now."

Dan shook his head. "Until I turned up, they'd done sweet FA."

"What does that mean? Sweet FA?"

"Sweet fuck all."

Lisa threw her head back and laughed. "Where did you learn that from?"

"Something the guys used to say in England."

"What, the soldiers?"

"Civilians too."

"Sweet FA. That's got to be my favorite Brit term of all time."

Lisa turned her attention back to the laptop. The broadband connection was slow. Google maps wouldn't upload. Lisa checked her modem and router. The laptop seemed to be working fine, but the green light in the router was flashing yellow.

"That normally means poor connection," Lisa said. "It's been like this the whole week. At work too, most of our computers are either down or working slowly."

"Let's get old school," Dan said. "You got any atlases?"

Lisa did. They took out a map and pored over the pages. Lisa found it. She stabbed her finger on a small point of the long coast where Georgia met the ocean.

"Here it is. Barnham."

"Just below St Mary's."

Lisa said, "St Mary is a nice little historic town. Popular tourist place."

Dan wanted to get going. But it was 1800 hours already and from the map it looked like a long, five-hour drive. The door bell sounded.

"You expecting someone?" he asked.

Lisa was biting her lower lip. "No."

Dan thought about the red Ford.

Twice, it had seen him near Lisa's apartment. Followed him around.

He went to his bag and took out the Sig. Lisa's eyes widened when she saw the weapon. Dan raised his finger to his lips and gestured. Lisa got up, took her laptop and went inside her bedroom. She opened the door a fraction and peeped out. Dan turned the lights out. In darkness, he stepped over to the door. He looked out through the door peep hole. It was a woman. Blonde hair. As she lifted her face, Dan felt the earth vanish from below his feet. His breath was suddenly coiled and tight in his chest.

It was Tanya.

Dan switched the lights back on. He opened the door and stared at Tanya for a second. Then he yanked her inside the apartment. Tanya stumbled inside. Her backpack was on her shoulder, and her hair was tied back in a pony-tail. She glared at Dan defiantly. Dan shut the door and put the Sig in his waistline.

"What do you think you're doing?" he hissed.

Tanya met his gaze. "He's my father. I'm not leaving him. I'll do whatever it takes."

Dan ran his hand over his face. "Tanya, I thought we agreed on this."

Tanya's eyes flashed. "Yes, we did. But then I thought about what was really going on. My dad would never leave me, if I was in trouble. He needs my help now. And I'll be there."

"Was it you in the red Ford?"

"I called one of my friends at the airport. She was nearby and we were lucky to catch you."

Dan's shoulder's dropped. "Oh, Tanya. What about your mom?"

"She's gone. She agreed to let me go when I told her I was going to come and see you."

"Hi there." Dan and Tanya whirled around as they heard Lisa's voice. The two women were staring at each other. Checking each other out. There was a long silence.

Dan said, "Lisa, this is Tanya…Philip Longworth's daughter."

Tanya asked, "Is this your girlfriend?" She looked at Dan crossly. "She knows about my dad too?"

Lisa said, "I am *not* his girlfriend. And I only recently found out about your father. I used to work with him.

Tanya said, "So, you knew my dad?"

"Yes," Lisa said. A look passed between the two women. Lisa added. "We knew each other as professional colleagues. Nothing else."

Tanya pointed to Dan and asked Lisa, "So, he's not your boyfriend, but he's still living with you?"

Dan intervened. "Tanya, Lisa was kind enough to offer me a place to sleep over till I found my own place."

The two women looked each other up and down again. Dan wiped his brow, wishing he had his handkerchief on him. Embarrassment fanned his face with heat.

"Lisa, I went to meet Tanya earlier today. Right now, she is meant to be on a flight." Dan narrowed his eyes at Tanya.

"Well," Lisa said. "She is *not* on a flight."

Dan said, "Can you please give us a minute?" He grabbed hold of Tanya's arm and steered her towards the door.

"Where are you going?" Lisa asked.

"I just need to speak to her. Back in a moment." He took Tanya out in the hallway, made sure he had the keys to the Lincoln, and shut the door.

He said, "Those two guys I killed today were the Russian Mafia. They are after you, because they think you might know where your dad is."

"I know that. Don't talk to me like I'm a child." Her chin came up.

"Did anyone follow you?"

"What? No."

"Are you sure?"

She paused, bravado all over her face. "Yes."

"Tanya, I know you think you're doing the right thing. I appreciate that. But believe me, this shit has hit the fan. The FBI and the Pentagon are involved. There's a lot more to this now than just your father disappearing. Today, his boss was killed."

"His boss?"

"Yes. The fat guy who came to your house. Him. Can you see? They're killing off the people close to him. Who do you think is next?"

She tried to shrug and act cool. But the flash in her eye was gone. "I don't care. Don't you get it? I love him. I can't just leave him out there. I…" her voice trembled slightly. "I also think he's sick. He lost a lot of weight in the last three months. Just like that. When I asked him, he said he joined a gym. He hates gyms."

Dan clenched his jaws and his fists. *Damn it. Damn you, Philip.*

Aloud, he said, "Let's go back to your dorm."

"My dorm?"

"Yes. To talk."

"I want to help you, Dan."

Dan held up his hands. "You have. And you will," he added hurriedly. "Just give me a chance to find out more. Then I'll call you. Promise me you won't follow me around anymore. It's just dangerous."

Her eyes were crafty. "Only if you promise you *will* call, and let me join you."

"I promise."

Tanya stayed in the elevator while Dan walked around the parking lot. A Honda Civic came in and parked. A woman got out, smiled at Dan and headed for the elevator. Dan signaled, and Tanya came out to join him. They got into the Lincoln.

"Give me your cell." Tanya frowned, but gave it to him. Dan turned the phone off and ripped out the battery. He gave both back to Tanya.

"Hey," she said. Dan took out his cell phone and did the same. They drove off into the gathering gloom of the close, humid evening. Orange, red and white lights were shining in the towers of downtown.

*****

Dan got back late, but Lisa was still awake. She was on the couch again, her arm draped over the side. Jimmy Fallon was cracking jokes on TV. She turned her head and gazed at Dan expectantly.

"What happened?"

"I found her another flight," Dan said, sounding relieved. He was. He wanted to crack open a beer, but this was not his home. "This time, I made sure I saw her board the damn thing."

"She did?"

"Yes, I even waited until the darned plane took off."

"So, what now?"

"Now we head for Barnham."

Dan was up early the next morning, packing the few belongings he had. He went through his yoga routine. Then he checked the Sig P226. He loaded the magazine full. It was all working fine. The Sig didn't have a safety catch. Instead it had a decocker. A round was always chambered and all he had to do was pull out the gun and fire. He liked that about the Sig. He put the gun in his front trouser pocket. Lisa knocked on his door. Her bag was a small suitcase.

"Got everything?" Dan asked.

She smiled sweetly. "Yup, including the bikini." She seemed more relaxed than yesterday, Dan thought. He drove the Lincoln to a gas station and filled it up. He checked the tire pressures. It was 0930 hours, and the morning traffic rush was subsiding. They headed out west and south, aiming for the I-75 to take them towards the sea.

After three hours of driving, Dan needed a break. They were approaching the seaside town of Savannah. He checked into a service station motel and they had lunch. The second leg of the journey was nicer. Dan wound his window down. The wind was fresher, less humid. He could see the blue glint of the Atlantic. It was past 1500 hours when they came off the I-75, and saw the first signs for Barnham town. The population was 120,000.

"Not as small as I thought," Dan said.

CHAPTER 27

Dan dropped his speed and they drove slowly into town. White shops and boutiques lined the main parade. Some of the houses were painted blue, red and yellow.

"Looks pretty," Lisa said.

"Where are we going?"

Dan took out a piece of paper.

"2334 Lynch Avenue, that's what Marcus's secretary told me. Hope she got it right."

"We need a town map," Dan said. He tried his phone again, but his, like Lisa's refused to upload Google maps. Dan pulled up at a motel and got a map from the reception counter. The seaside was next to the main town parade. He parked the Lincoln at the nearest lot and they both got out and stretched. The sun was shining on the sea. Seagulls soared overhead. The air was heavy with saline mist. Dan stared at the sparkling water. It was beautiful being this close to the sea again.

Dan spread the map out on the hood. There was an A to Z at the back. He found the street name, and then got it on the map. He took out a pen and circled it. It was further in from the main parade. He turned to Lisa.

"You need a place to stay." She pointed at the motel. "It looks alright."

Dan shrugged. They got back inside the car and drove. The motel was big, new and shiny. It was called Motel 10, and was over two floors. Rooms radiated across a balcony on each floor. There was a large parking lot in front. They parked, took their bags and went inside. The large reception area was mostly empty. A small Indian man was sitting behind the desk, his eyes on a computer screen. Above him a sign said "Sea view rooms with free views."

As Lisa and Dan approached the man clicked his tongue and shook his head. He took his eyes off the screen and looked at them. His lips split into a smile.

"Hello, welcome to Motel 10."

They signed in for a double room. The reception man turned his attention to the screen again. "Darned broadband not working again."

Dan said, "Problem here as well?"

"Most of Georgia, it seems. Where have you guys come from?"

"Atlanta."

The man shook his head. "So slow it's easier to just pick up the phone and ask someone." He looked at Dan curiously. "Any problems there with the internet?"

"Slow as you have it down here."

"God knows what's going on." The man picked up some keys. "Let me show you to your rooms."

Dan picked up the bags. They took the stairs up to the first floor. The sea sparkled between the trees in the distance. When they were inside and the man had left, Dan stood by the door with his bag in his hands. Lisa went over to the sliding glass door and checked out the balcony overlooking the sea. She came back and stared at him.

"What are you doing?"

"I'm going to check out a few things. See you soon."

"Hang on. I'm coming with you."

Dan shook his head. "No. Too dangerous. I'm sure they're here. Keep your phone on, I'll call."

He went out the door, down the stairs, and checked the location of Lynch Avenue with the motel keeper once. In the parking lot, he opened the trunk of the Lincoln and put his bag in. He stuck the Sig inside his front belt, next to the knife. He got into the car and looked around him. The parking lot had three cars excluding his. One Dodge van, a pick up, and a Honda coupe. He hadn't seen any of the cars before. If someone was following him, they were doing one hell of a good job. That, or they were waiting for him.

He stopped at a service station, refueled, and bought a bacon cheese burger, two cans of soda, a packet of cookies and a takeaway coffee. He ate the burger and drank the coffee in the car.

He followed the map up to Lynch Avenue, but didn't go into the street.

He circled around. The avenue was on a crisscross grid of streets at the top of a hill that overlooked the ocean. It was windy and fresh. He parked the car two streets down, under a tree. He walked past Lynch Avenue twice, noting the parked cars and any pedestrians. The street was empty. Mostly rental holiday homes, he guessed.

As he walked back on one of his circles, the blue ocean faced him. He could see a white ship with its stern open, a large crane on its deck raised like a question mark. The crane had a pulley that was revolving, laying something on the water. A fishing trawler, he guessed. But from this distance he could not see clearly.

He walked into Lynch Avenue after a while and headed for number 2334. The property was similar to most on the street. Two-story, post-colonial, with warm colors. Steps went up to a wood porch with an empty recliner. The two houses on either side had cars in the drive. As he watched a man came out, smiled at Dan, and got into the car. Dan watched as the man reversed out, then he walked up the drive. He waited until the car had gone before he rang the bell. The bell chimed. Twice. There was no answer. He knocked. No response.

He came down the porch stairs and down the side. The garden went to the edge of the hill then slid down after a fence. Dan tried the back entrance. He peered in through the window, it was the kitchen door. The door was locked. He hadn't seen an alarm at the front wall or the back. He took out the knife and his credit card. He kneeled down and jiggled the lock with the knife, while trying for the bolt with the credit card. After five minutes of trying he gave up.

He got up and looked around. The houses on either side couldn't see him. He leaned against the door, then pushed. He pushed harder, and with a crack, the lock split from the door frame. He tensed himself for an alarm he hadn't seen, but there was no sound. He breathed easy and let the door swing inside. He waited for a beat, then stepped inside. It was dead quiet.

The kitchen was medium-sized. Two dishes rested in the sink. The cupboards were all open. Plates, pots and pans had been dragged out and lay in a heap on the floor. The dining table in the middle was overturned. One of the chairs had its leg broken. He took out his Sig. He stepped around the mess until he came out in the hallway. Carpets had been ripped up, showing bare floorboards. He checked the living room. Two sofas upturned, foam slashed in broad knife strokes. Similar to Philip's house. He kept the gun raised and crept upstairs. Same carnage. Carpets lifted, floorboards loose. There were three bedrooms upstairs, of which only one was used. All the doors were open; every room had been trashed. Dan put his gun away.

He looked around the house and found nothing. On the upstairs landing, he checked the window facing the street. The neighbor he had seen leaving was parking his car in the drive again. He looked up and down the street and saw something new. A black Cadillac. Parked three houses down to the left, on the opposite side. He could see two men in the front. Maybe more in the back. The men sat there, watching.

Dan came away from the window. He went downstairs and opened the main door. The porch creaked under his trunks. He looked at the neighbor by his car. He was closing the trunk. Dan glanced at the Cadillac. Four guys at the very least. Staring directly at him. He walked over to the neighbor, a middle-aged man with light grey and white hair. The man stopped as Dan approached.

"Hello there," Dan said. He jerked a thumb towards the house. "Here to see Philip Longworth. He used to live there."

The neighbor thought for a while. Then his eyes cleared. "Ah, yes. To be honest, a few people come and go from that house every year. It's a rental home. But I remember the last guy there. If that's who you mean. What did he look like?"

Dan took out the photo of Philip with his family on the hiking trail. The one he had taken from Philip's study.

"Yes," the neighbor said. "That's him. How do you know him?"

"A friend of the family." The rest he didn't need to know.

"I see. You know, I gotta mention it, he seemed kinda odd. Kept to himself. Tall chap, and always walked bent over. Quite pale. Was he sick?"

Dan nodded, keeping his face straight. "Yes, he was. Do you remember anything particular about him? Like his car, or what time he came home from work. Anything really."

"Well, he never had a car. He always took the bus from the end of the road, where it joins the Corinthian Road. That's the main road that heads down to St Mary's."

"Okay, did he take the bus every morning?"

"I reckon so, yes. Came home pretty late I guess, I never saw him."

"Did he have visitors?"

The man shook his head. "No, he was a loner."

"You live here alone?"

"No, with my wife. Kids are in college. You're welcome to ask her, but she wouldn't have seen anything else."

"Thank you," Dan said. "By any chance, you wouldn't know which bus he took, would you?"

"As a matter of fact, I do. I drove past him a few times as he was boarding it. He took Number 37. That goes to town and does a loop back here."

"Thanks, you've been a big help."

Dan glanced over the man's shoulder. The Cadillac was still there. He returned to the Lincoln and drove off. He took the main road back to the motel by the Broadway. A check on the rear-view mirror confirmed it—the Cadillac was following him. He drove inside the parking lot of the motel, and as he parked, the Cadillac flashed past. The passenger side window was lowered and a blond-haired man was staring out. They caught each other's eyes.

CHAPTER 28

Dan went inside the motel. It was the same guy at reception. There was a TV above the counter as well and CNN was on. Three people were standing around and listening to the news. Dan watched. The senator whose emails had been hacked had resigned.

Opposition lawyers were pressing charges against him. The senator had links with Russian criminals who were close to powerful figures in Kremlin. Capitol Hill was in uproar. The hacker was still mysteriously absent. The two parties were blaming each other and Congress had come to a standstill as first the Democrat, then the Republican senators had walked out.

Dan shook his head. The whole thing was a big mess. The three men who Dan thought were guests looked at him and moved back. The Indian guy behind the counter smirked at Dan.

"See what these idiots are up to?"

"Like Dumb and Dumber," Dan said. "I need to find the Town Hall. Do you know where it is?"

Dan got the directions and went back to the car. He thought of checking on Lisa, but figured she would be either be resting or getting a tan on the balcony. He opened the trunk, and took extra ammunition for the Sig. He had a feeling he was going to need it soon.

After ten minutes of driving he was out on a country lane. Farmland appeared on the left and the ocean to the right. He saw the white ship again, the crane on its deck, and some other machinery. He drove on and came into a small complex. It had the town hall and sheriff's office. He pulled into the parking lot of the town hall. A bored-looking woman at the reception looked up as he entered. She was in her fifties, red hair tied up in a bun at the back, eyes behind thick-rimmed glasses that looked at Dan blankly.

"Can I help you?" she asked.

"Yes, there's an internet cable project going on here. A company called

Synchrony Communications is in charge. They're based in Atlanta. I need to speak to someone dealing with them."

"What for?"

Dan put his elbows on the counter and leaned over. "The man Synchrony sent over has disappeared. The cops are looking for him. He's my friend and I'm here to look for him. Now if you don't mind, I need to speak to someone who knows more about this."

The woman reached for the phone. "Have a seat there, please. Let me see who I can get for you."

"You do that," Dan said.

He sat down on a worn leather sofa by the window, looking at the ocean sparkling in the distance like gems had been scattered on the water. A bunch of cars were parked in the parking lot. The land beyond dipped over a hill. He could see the white ship ploughing the water far away. Dan became aware of a presence beside him. He looked up to see a pot-bellied, middle-aged man standing with a curious look on his face. Dan stood up. The man took a step back, then composed himself.

"I'm Richard Maxwell. In charge of town infrastructure planning. I understand you need to speak to someone about Synchrony Communications."

"Yes." Dan introduced himself and they shook hands.

"Please, come into my office."

They sat down in the air-conditioned office, facing each other.

"How can I help you?" Maxwell asked. Dan told him about Philip.

"Did you meet him?" Dan asked.

"Once in the beginning, yes. After that, he got busy with the project and we never saw each other again. What do the police think is happening?"

"They're still looking for clues," Dan said. Maxwell had seen better days. The flesh on his cheeks hung loosely over his jowls, his hair was almost nonexistent, and he had a tired hang-dog expression.

Dan said, "Did you know that the CEO of Synchrony Communications has died?"

Maxwell blinked and controlled himself. "He died?"

Dan was suddenly wary. Maxwell knew something and he was hiding it, just like Marcus Schopp had done.

"Shot dead in his car. Two bullets to the head. The evening before, he told me if I didn't stop looking for Philip, I would get everyone killed."

Maxwell looked around the room like a trapped animal. He licked his lips.

"That's strange. I mean, I don't know why…" He looked at Dan. "Why are you telling me this?"

"Because I'm trying to find Philip. Tell me about this project, Mr. Maxwell. Is it about broadband cables or something else?"

Maxwell didn't answer. Dan said, "Philip's house in Atlanta and the place he rented over here have both been trashed. Like someone was looking for something. You know anything about that?"

Maxwell stood up and pulled the blinds down. He folded his hands on the desk.

"Look, I don't know who you are. I don't know what happened to Philip. This project is like others up and down the country, nothing special."

"Why does a defense military contractor handle a civilian infrastructure project like this?" Dan asked.

Maxwell closed his eyes and opened them, like he was exhausted. When he spoke, his voice croaked.

"Mr. Roy, there is nothing else I can tell you. If you visit our website, there is enough information about the project."

Dan stood up. "Remember what happened to Marcus, Mr. Maxwell. Might be better if you came clean with me now."

"Goodbye, Mr. Roy."

Outside, Dan pulled his cell phone out and called Andy Brown.

"Any news on Marcus?" Dan asked.

"Something came up from his previous records. He used to work for DARPA," Andy said.

"That research place?"

"Defense Advanced Research Projects Agency. It's like the NASA for the military. They build on ideas from scientists and defense contractors by providing funding. They came up with stuff like the stealth planes and the miniature GPS you can put in a phone."

Dan remembered an old article in a military gadgets magazine. "Yeah, I got it. So, what did Marcus do for them?"

"It gets a bit vague there. It says he was the office supervisor for a branch of the Tactical Technology Office in Atlanta. Then he left and opened up Synchrony."

"Alright. Listen, I need your help with something."

"Shoot."

"I don't know if you intended that pun, but that's precisely what I might need. If it gets rough down here I might need a hand. Is it cool for you to come down here? I have a feeling Philip is somewhere around."

"Maybe. Let me check with the chief. If it's for this case, she might be okay with it."

Dan hung up and went into the police station. If Barnham had a problem with crime, it didn't show in its offices. Dan had never visited a more pristine, well-organized police station. It felt like an office block. The air conditioner hummed out cool air, the walls were covered in nice paintings, the seats were leather and comfortable. A uniformed man was at the counter. He carried on writing something until Dan was right up at the desk.

"This the right place to ask about a missing person?" Dan said. The police officer was in his late twenties to early thirties. He had black hair and a pale complexion that had turned ruddy in the coastal sun. His dark eyes stared back at Dan.

"Has a report been filed?" he asked.

"Philip Longworth. Atlanta PD should have been in touch."

The policeman picked up his coffee and tapped a few buttons on his computer.

"Yes," he said eventually. "Philip Longworth of 2334 Lynch Avenue. That correct?"

"Yup. Any news?"

The man grimaced and stretched his arms, like he had all the time in the world. "Nope. We get them once in a while."

Once in a while, Dan thought. "Do their houses get trashed and their bosses get killed once in a while, as well?"

That got his attention. "Say what?"

"You got a police chief here?"

The chief's office was at the back, surrounded by cactus and other long leaf green plants in pots. Dan stood while the sulky young man knocked on the door. A sign on the glass panel said, Greg Radomski, Police Chief, Barnham Town. The police officer shut the door, leaving Dan outside. In a few minutes, he came back out.

"He'll see you now." He jerked a thumb towards the office.

A broad-shouldered, beefy man sat at the desk. He looked at Dan without smiling and didn't offer to shake his hand.

"Who are you?" Chief Radomski asked.

Dan told him. He repeated what he had told the young officer, and left out everything in between. He mentioned Brown in Atlanta. Radomski grunted.

"You see a connection between his boss's murder and his disappearance?"

Dan said, "I went to ask him myself. He was evasive. He died the next day."

Radomski said, "We mounted a county-wide patrol car search for him. Showed his photo to residents. Radio and TV ads. Found nothing so far. And now the internet is playing up. Things are slow."

"Nothing so far?"

"Zip."

Dan changed tack. "What do you know about the broadband cable job?"

Radomski curled up his nose. "Far as I knew we had broadband already. Folks in the town hall were vague about it. I figured it was something political, so I stayed out of it."

Vagueness was exactly what he got from Maxwell, but evasion, too. The man had fobbed him off. Looks like he had fobbed the police off as well. It wouldn't be hard. In a small town, an infrastructure project meant jobs.

"You know where Philip worked around here?"

"Sure. By the water. Take the Corinthian Road towards St Mary's."

"Yeah, I heard." A thought struck Dan. "St Mary's is close to the King's Bay submarine base, isn't it?"

"Yes. Nuclear submarine base. Cumberland Island is close by. You been there? Nice place. Got wild horses and shit."

Dan's eyes flared. A sudden memory hit the sides of his skull like an explosion, blowing every other thought apart. He caught his breath.

"What did you say?"

Radomski stopped when he caught the look in Dan's eyes. "About the submarine base?"

Dan's voice was urgent. "No, about the horses."

"Oh, that's Cumberland Island. The place has wild horses that no one gets close to. They bite and stuff."

"Goodbye, Chief. I'll be in touch."

CHAPTER 29

Dan drove fast. Streets flashed past on his right, with the ocean opposite. The white ship had come into the harbor, berthed offshore.

The horse's neighs.

The sound that Tanya had heard when Philip had called her.

The place had been windy, probably a beach. Philip was in Cumberland Island. He knew the hiking trails well. The family went there regularly. Philip would know where to hide.

Dan looked in his rear-view mirror. He had company. The Cadillac and another car were following about fifty meters behind. Dan pressed on the gas, pushing the needle up to a hundred. The Lincoln surged in response. The Cadillac was keeping pace, and if anything, getting closer. Dan pushed the speed past one hundred and ten. The Lincoln and the car directly behind speeded up, too.

The Cadillac was more powerful. The Lincoln was a town car, but Dan guessed from the Cadillac's shape it was a sports model. As he watched, the Cadillac moved out to the empty lane on the left and accelerated. Dan realized their plan. The Cadillac was trying to outflank him. Behind him, the other car leapt into view in the rear-view mirror. It was a blue Chrysler. The car came closer and Dan could see the red bandana of the driver. The Z9 gang. The Mexican gang-banger he had seen in the warehouse in Marietta. Dan reached into the glove box and put his phone in his shirt pocket.

They would try to force him off the road.

The Cadillac moved closer. Dan could hear the growl of its engine. The driver he didn't recognize, but the passenger was tall and blond. Dan took his foot off the accelerator and pulled the Sig out. He lowered the window on the passenger side. The wind roared inside the Lincoln, bringing dust and sand, and Dan blinked as some of it went into his eyes.

He drove with his left hand. On his right hand, he held the Sig, balanced against his other forearm. Dan fired twice, quickly. The Cadillac's driver's window shattered. The car went forward, swerving on the road. Then it overtook Dan and began to slow down. Dan wound down his window and fired another two shots, aiming for the rear tires. Behind him he heard a crashing sound and he ducked down in his seat. The Mexicans were firing at him.

Bullets popped in the back and his rear wind screen smashed into a thousand shards of glass. The Chrysler moved forward.

Dan was trapped. The Cadillac ahead of him was slowing him down, and the Chrysler behind him was moving in for the kill. He crouched as low as he could and gritted his teeth. He jolted as his front bumper smashed against the Cadillac's rear. He made up his mind up in an instant. He swung the wheel a hard left.

The Lincoln's tires skidded and the front bumpers ground against the Cadillac, metal tearing against metal. The car came off the road onto the dirt. Dust flew in through the open windows, blinding him momentarily. Dan wrenched the wheel back straight, then to the left again. He wanted to raise up more dust. The trees weren't far away now, a row of tall, old oaks up ahead. He screeched to a stop in a cloud of dust. He could hear the whine of tires against asphalt as the other cars braked and came off the road.

Dan kicked open the passenger side door and slid out head-first. He rolled on the ground and was up in an instant. Using the car as a shield, he shot three times at the Chrysler, and three more towards the Russians. Visibility was poor in the dust swirl and he could barely make out the shapes. He heard two screams from the Russian car.

Then he turned and ran, diving into the trees.

The foliage was dense. Shrubs covered the ground and the trees were wet with moss. He knew the ocean was close, but he couldn't see it. Daylight became shaded as he went deeper. He could hear shouts behind him. He stopped for a moment behind the trunk of a thick oak. No dog barks. That was good. A dog would have moved much quicker through the forest than a human. He heard another shout, an order to spread out. He ran again, moving swiftly between the trees. He wanted to stop and shoot, but he needed distance from them first, and shooting would give his position away too quickly.

As he ran, he considered the numbers. Four in each car. Eight against one at a minimum. Could be more. He had hit one, maybe. He could take down some more, but they could outflank him.

He stopped. The trees in front were getting lighter and ahead of him he could see sand dunes. Beyond that, the sea. He could hide in the sand dunes. But after that, all he had was the open beach. He didn't like the idea of a firefight on an open beach. He could bog them down on the sand dunes. He had four extra clips of ammo on him. But so would they.

The forest stretched out in either direction. He couldn't hear them anymore. He ran again, flitting between the trees. They had spread out and the farther he went, the more chances he had of coming up on one of them alone. He liked the forest terrain. It gave him options. Twice, he heard a sound and dropped to the ground, crawling on his elbows. Nobody. He kept up this routine of hiding, listening, running until sweat covered his body.

He paused for rest behind a tree and looked. The ground was dry and he was careful not to step on branches. A sound grabbed his attention. Five o'clock. A man, moving slowly between the trees. His gun arm was hanging by his side and he had lit a cigarette. Dan crouched low and looked behind him to the other side. In the distance, he could see another figure. Eight o'clock. But he was further away.

Dan put the Sig into his pocket and took the knife out. He flicked it open. There was a fallen tree and he lay down flat behind it. His shirt was getting wet from the moss. When he looked up, the man diagonally to his right had moved up. Twenty meters, at the most. Still smoking his cigarette. Careless. Dan let him pass by. Then he slithered over the tree and followed.

He came closer. When Dan was two meters behind him, the man stumbled against a tree trunk. He cursed and began to straighten himself. Dan crept up behind him and put his hand over the mouth, pulling the man into his chest. In the same movement the serrated edge of the curved knife slid inside the anterior angle of the neck, above the neck muscles. It destroyed the trachea, shred the carotid artery and jugular vein and crushed the soft bones of the sinuses. Blood spurted through the nose and mouth. Dan twisted the knife once, grinding deeper into the lower skull. The body twitched and jerked, but he held it steady. Then he lowered it gently to the ground. He wiped his arm on the man's pants. He was carrying a Smith Wesson 0.357. Dan pocketed the gun.

The forest was silent, save the chirping of birds high above. Dan ran behind a tree and looked around. He couldn't see the man to his left anymore. He guessed he had moved up ahead. Dan ran from tree to tree again, keeping low. He retraced his path, running back towards the car. By now, the gangsters would be near the sand dune, facing the ocean. Soon, they would realize that Dan wasn't there. Then they would head back. Dan kept up his routine of hiding and running. In five minutes, he was near the road. He could see the three cars between the trees. He dropped to the ground and observed.

Movement. Next to the Cadillac. He saw the barrel of a gun.

CHAPTER 30

An M4 assault rifle, hung from the shoulder of a man who came around the Cadillac. He put his feet apart and stared at the forest. Bad news. If that gun went off, someone would hear the sound. But the man had one serious disadvantage. He was out in the open ground. He had no shelter. To a sniper, he was dead meat. Moments like these, Dan missed his Heckler and Koch 417 rifle. But he had the Sig, and he had a 357 round chambered in it. Nice, heavy ordnance. Dan stayed low and got into range.

The man was to his right, two o'clock. He had the rifle ready, and he was staring straight ahead. Dan stayed flat on the ground and took out the handgun. He held it in both hands, elbows straight, finger on the trigger. He had to aim between the trees. He had to hurry up too, if the man moved he would miss his mark. He slowed his breathing. He was less than forty meters away. Dan increased pressure on the trigger. The man moved. He turned his head, then his body, and looked straight towards Dan. Dan was spread-eagled on the ground, and the man's view passed over him. Dan swore and adjusted. Now or never. He fired.

The round slammed into the mouth and exited out the back of the skull, blowing the back of the head away. A gust of red mist and bone fragments, and the body slumped to the ground. Dan was on his feet and moving before the body hit the ground. He picked up the M4, searched quickly for extra ammo, which he found in the front of the dead man's jacket. He took out his knife and ran to the Chrysler. He plunged the knife in the two rear tires, and did the same to the Lincoln.

He jerked his head up as he heard a sound. Behind him. Feet crunching leaves. They were coming back. Dan ran to the front of the Cadillac. The keys were in the ignition. He slid the M4 on the passenger side seat and jumped in. The engine growled. There were shouts and screams, and he ducked as he heard the whine of a round. Then came the chatter of automatic fire. Dan pressed on the gas and turned the wheel.

The car leaped up the road and behind him, there was an explosion. It was one of the rear tires. They were shooting for it. Dan drove desperately, but there was another explosion and a black cloud engulfed the vehicle. The second rear tire and the exhaust gone. Dan could feel the drag as the car slowed, despite him pushing the gas pedal to metal.

He didn't have many options. He checked the lane opposite. A pick up whizzed by, then the lane was empty. Dan picked up the M4, checked his Sig and the Smith and Wesson, made sure the knife was still tucked into his belt. With the car still running, he opened the driver's side door and turned the steering wheel.

With screeches of protest, the burst tires flapped on the asphalt. The car turned around in a semi-circle. He jammed on the brakes and tumbled out of the seat onto the road. Bullets were slamming into the car, but he had the car as a shield between him and the gangsters. He counted six of them. All had their handguns raised and were firing at will. There was another explosion as one of the front tires burst. The men were spread out in a line. Dan aimed with the M4 and picked out the man in the middle. He was wearing the red bandana. He double-tapped him on the head and chest and the man crumpled to the ground.

The firing got heavy. As bullets whizzed overhead he crept out the side of the car, staying low. As he had expected, one of the men on the right was trying to move in. A quick burst felled him. Four still approaching.

Dan rolled over to the other side of the car. A bullet found the window above him and showered him with glass. He shook his head free of the fragments. He located the man on the extreme left this time. The gangster had his gun raised firing at the car. But he wasn't pointing low, where Dan was hiding, and he wasn't watching his shots. Two head shots dropped him dead. Three left.

Dan quickly did a Sit Rep. It was one of the worst things in combat, not to have circumferential awareness. If they had more than eight, one or two could easily have gone around and shot him in the back. In front of him, several bullets slammed into the hood of the car and picked up puffs of dust on the asphalt on the side.

Movement from the other side. Shit. Shit.

Dan saw a shadow flit through the trees to his right. Behind him. With his back to the car, Dan lifted the gun and aimed. Four o'clock. He didn't switch the rifle to automatic. He let off three shots and he saw the shadow fall. Then it got back up again and ran forwards. Dan whirled to the opposite side. Goddamn. Another shadow, running fast. Eight o'clock. They had managed to outflank him. There was no escape. He lifted the M4, aiming for the man on the left.

Then he stopped. The man carried a rifle, but it wasn't aimed at him. As Dan watched, the man fired directly over Dan's head, towards the gangsters. Dan heard a sound and looked up. He knew that sound very well. The rotor blades of a helicopter.

The bird flew in from the ocean, staying well above firing range. It hovered above, then swept across, blades flashing in the sun. Dan whirled his head left and right. He couldn't hear firing from the gangsters anymore. Two black shadows emerged from the trees. On each side. Four in total. They approached in arrow formation, ten meters behind each other, guns trained on Dan. They all had beards, about two to three month's growth.

"Put your weapon down," the lead man on the right shouted. Dan looked at him carefully. Black combat pants and top. Knee pads for sniping. The rifle looked like a suppressed Hecker and Koch. Microphone in one ear. Handgun in thigh holster. Kevlar vest and fragmentation grenades on the belt. These were not gangsters, nor were they rank and file soldiers. He didn't have a hope in hell.

"Put the gun down," the man shouted again. They were ten meters away now. Dan saw the two men at the back peel off to the sides and advance towards the gangsters. He couldn't hear a peep from behind him.

It was suddenly deathly quiet. A breeze rushed in through the trees. Dan put the M4 down. He lifted up his hands. He turned on his knees and stayed like that, arms spread up. The two front men approached him. One of them searched Dan for weapons and removed the two hand guns and the knife. The other kept his rifle on Dan's face. He motioned with his rifle, and Dan stood up slowly. He patted Dan down, then stood back and shoved him forward. Dan stumbled, but kept his balance.

The two who had recced out to the sides came back. Dan hadn't heard any further shots. The surviving gangsters had escaped, or they were dead. The four men circled Dan, each with their rifles trained on him, fingers on triggers. Dan didn't lower his hands.

"My name is Dan Roy," he said. "I could be wrong, but I think I'm on the same side as you."

"Shut the fuck up," the lead man said. He lowered Dan's hands and tied them in a plastic handcuff. He produced a cloth bag and draped it over Dan's head. The world turned black before Dan's eyes. It was hard to breathe. He felt a rifle prod him in the back.

"Move," a voice barked.

CHAPTER 31

"There, there it is!" Shevchenko tried to keep the excitement from his voice, but failed. Both the *Krasnaya* and the *Gobuki* were down at the sea bed today. Sasha craned his neck to look at the large screen above the scientists' head. The picture quality was excellent. The screen showed the fiber optic cable that carried information from the east coast of USA to mainland Europe. This particular cable was brand new, having taken more than a year and almost a billion dollars to complete. Its landing station was in Jacksonville, Florida and on the other side, almost four thousand miles away, in the northern coast of France.

They had found the cable three days ago. Right now, their main source of excitement was the object that had detached itself from a console on the side of the *Gobuki* and fixed itself like a hook on the cable. It was a clip-on coupler, a type widely available commercially, routinely used to check signal in the fiber and ensure internet traffic, including voice and video communication flows optimally.

They were also used for eavesdropping, often in the name of network maintenance.

But this coupler was different. It had a robotic arm that made the hook around the cable into a saw. That saw was now being used to cut into the reinforced steel casing that covered the large bundle of optic fibers that carried internet signals from USA to Europe.

Shevchenko leaned back in his seat, a satisfied smile on his face. The most gratifying thing was that the transducers had been bought on Ebay, the coupler from a New Jersey company, and then modified with the robotic arms at a secret lab in Moscow.

He watched on the screen as the saw cut into the steel, with flashes of yellow sparks. Soon smoke covered the screen. Shevchenko lifted a hand.

"Stop," he commanded. He waited for the ocean currents to clear the smoke. The others leaned forward around him. The steel casing had fallen apart, and inside the nerve like cords of fibers lay exposed. The two arms of the robotic device were poised above them.

Shevchenko rubbed his hands together. "Comrades, now we start. No more than ten fibers at a time. If we chop the whole thing off, the alarm will be raised quickly. No, we want the Imperialists to suffer."

Sasha whispered, "Block by block, city by city, we shall make their screens go blank."

"That's the plan, my boy. Now let's get to it. *Bistra!*"

Shevchenko watched as the pincer like claws of the arms grabbed a cluster of fibers, and began to bend them.

His mind went back to the hacking operation. It had taken them a week to sort through all the data. Then the Democrat Head Office emails were hacked. From there, getting into a Republican senator's emails hadn't been difficult. One thing the coupler couldn't do was transmit information. Wi-Fi was impossible under water, although work was progressing towards achieving that. From an office in Sporchivniya, Moscow, bogus emails from Russian businessmen were filling the mail inbox of this senator. Shevchenko almost felt sorry for the man.

But worse was to come. When the final information arrived, then the *Krasnaya* and the *Gobuki*—the Russian Navy's premier unmanned undersea vehicles or UUV's—would go into combat mode. No, they couldn't start a war. But they could disrupt the American plans. Simple sabotage in multiple places would go a long way. Shevchenko wasn't really interested in these cables.

The real game awaited them.

He breathed out with impatience as he thought of the delay. Despite how the Kremlin had vouched for their agent, Shevchenko wasn't convinced. These agents, assets, spies, whatever one wanted to call them, always ended up either getting caught or blabbing their secrets. Take that Edward Snowden, for instance. If he was Russian, would he even be alive today?

Impulsively, he checked his cell phone. No calls. No SMS. Still waiting. He was about to yawn when the alarm sounded, almost knocking him off his chair. The two scientists jumped and removed their headphones. Shevchenko went out the door onto the bridge. Men were running on the deck outside. He noticed a figure rushing out of the sonar receiver on the aft deck. Shevchenko shimmied down the staircase and fought his way out on the open deck. A man saluted.

"What is it?" Shevchenko demanded. "And shut that damned alarm off. It's not like we have been hit by a torpedo."

"Sir, it's the telescopes. And it's been confirmed by our satellite feed trying to jam their GPS frequency. There's an American plane over us."

Shevchenko craned his neck up, but couldn't see anything. It was what Shevchenko had feared. It was what the idiots in Kremlin, and the dumb ass criminal this agent was forcing him to rely on, would never understand.

Durakh, he thought bitterly. *Durakh*. Stupid idiots.

He hurried to the telescope chamber and looked through them. He spotted the thing finally. He magnified the image. It was a long plane with a huge wingspan. Grey in color, with white numbers on it. He had seen this plane's images on recon photos in the past.

"A Poseidon P8A plane. Belongs to the US Navy," he muttered to himself. He felt a presence behind him. It was Sasha. He asked, "Any updates?"

"Yes, Captain. Sonobouys were dropped from the aircraft at 1310 hours. It is 1312 now."

"Sonobuoys," Shevchenko repeated. Passive sonar receivers to catch their sound waves. Sonobuoys were very versatile and could fire sound waves as well, using their echo to build an image of what they were hitting.

He told Sasha, "It is possible they have been watching us for a while. We probably have a drone on top as we speak. That does not worry me. The drone cannot see through the titanium roof of the dry dock. But I don't know how powerful these sonobouys are. If they can get a glimpse of our UUV then we are done for."

There was a shout from the bridge. It became persistent. A sailor rushed in, sweat pouring down his face.

"Sir, the scientists want to see you."

Shevchenko and Sasha dashed upstairs. Pavel pointed at the screen as they burst into the control room.

"This just came back from our pencil beam sonar collision avoidance system on the *Gobuki*," Pavel said. Shevchenko peered closely at the screen. The pencil beam sent out sound waves to see if there was any object in its way. The vehicle caught the echo coming off any obstruction, and then navigated around it. But the data it sent back was grainy and vague. It was something large, whatever it was.

"Could it be the continental shelf, Captain?" Pavel suggested.

Shevchenko scrunched his face. Something disturbing was lurking at the back of his mind. "Turn the collision systems off. From now on, we do not send any active sonar out."

He left the scientists and went to the sonar technician's office. They were sat hunched over the assortment of screen in front of them, eyes moving, a blue glow on their faces. He tapped Yuri on the shoulder.

"Did you keep a record of those small sounds you picked up?"

"Yes, Captain." He flicked back through the screens to bring up the images. He laid them out in rows on a large display.

"Can you get the time these sounds appear?" he asked Yuri. The man pressed a few keys and the data came up.

Shevchenko pointed to the screen. "Can you see the pattern? These sounds occur at morning and…" he stopped. Yuri looked at him, his mouth open. The senior technician knew perfectly what his Captain was saying. Blood drained from Shevchenko's face. Beads of sweat formed on his forehead.

"These are transient sounds. From a submarine." He didn't have to explain any further to Yuri.

Both nuclear and diesel submarines were known for being very quiet. Their propellers and engines hardly made any sound. They could never be picked up by passive sonar. But the sounds the crew made—banging toilet seats down, walking around, washing—all of these sounds produced detectable sound waves. So called transient sounds were often what gave a submarine's position away.

"They are here. I think it's an Ohio class nuclear one, stationed at the Kings Bay Naval Yard." Shevchenko swallowed hard. "Sasha, get those UUV's out of the water right now. They might engage us." He set his face in a grim look. "Prepare our torpedoes. If they make adverse contact, then we respond with force. I am not surrendering this ship."

Sasha's eyes were wide. "But Captain, that means…"

Shevchenko stared at his protégé. "Yes, Sasha. It means war. Now get the torpedoes ready, and get Kremlin on the satellite phone for me."

CHAPTER 32

Dan stumbled along the ground, his feet kicking small pebbles. The barrel of the rifle jammed into his back frequently. He couldn't see anything and breathing was difficult with the bag over his face. It was ironic that he had used similar methods when he had captured insurgents in Iraq and Afghanistan. He wondered what sort of interrogation he would be subjected to, and if they would employ so-called advanced techniques. Dan had been trained both to interrogate and resist questioning. He hoped like hell he would not have to use any of those skills now.

He listened hard. These guys had saved him. Why? Did they think he knew something? If they did, then he would definitely be facing advanced techniques. Which would also mean they were the enemy.

Well, he sure as hell wouldn't be telling them a word. He would rather die. Slowly, if necessary.

He could hear the birds again. It was darker. They must be in the forest. The ground became crunchy with fallen leaves and branches. A wind picked up, blowing the cloth against his face. Sea salt. A moment later, he heard the sound of surf. His trunks sank into something soft and warm. Sand. They were on the beach. The sand became firmer after a while and they kept walking. The team pushed him until he was walking on something harder. Felt like duck planks laid along a beach. They turned away from the ocean and he felt the wind on his back now. His head was pressed down and he guessed it was to go through a doorway. He hesitated for a second, but there was no point in resisting.

A door slammed and it was pitch black. A light came on, bright even against his covered eyes. He was pushed, and judging by the sounds, he was in a narrow hallway. They kept moving until he was finally shoved into a room. The bag was lifted from his eyes. The room was dark, but it was still daylight outside. A small grill window let in sunlight. Dan blinked until his eyes got used to the light. He looked around the room. A heavy steel door was open at the front. One of the men with stood there with his rifle down, but trigger finger on guard. He looked at Dan, his face devoid of expression. There was another man in the room with him. He had short ginger hair, and freckles covered his face and forearms. It was the same man who had cuffed him. He stood behind Dan and unlocked the handcuffs. He stepped back. Dan turned around slowly.

The man had a gun pointed at Dan's belly.

"Any trouble and we shoot you first, ask questions later. Do you understand?"

Dan cleared his throat. "Yes."

The man went out, keeping his gun trained on Dan. He slammed the door shut and keys turned in the lock. Dan staggered back against the cold wall. It was made of metal, probably steel. There was a musty smell inside, which the tiny grill window at the top did nothing to relieve. He sat down and massaged his wrists. His throat was parched dry. He wiped the sweat off his brow and lay down on the cold floor. He tried to sleep, feeling thirstier than he had ever done in his life.

It was 1700 hours. After fifteen minutes, he heard a key turn in the lock. A man he had never seen before came in. He was younger, clean shaven, and wore a navy working uniform. He carried a tray of food. Behind him, one of the bearded men came in and pointed his rifle at Dan. Dan grabbed the bottle of water on the tray and chugged it down in one gulp. He looked at the food and grimaced.

"Oh man, not an MRE," Dan said. They tasted horrid, but as in a combat situation, he had little choice now. He grabbed the packet.

The MRE was black bean and rice burritos. The packet had dried peaches, a fruit bar, pan cakes and the burrito. It wasn't that bad. He hadn't eaten since that morning and an MRE had never tasted this good. Not when he was on holiday, anyway. He leaned back against the wall. They had taken his cell. Even without the battery, he had no doubt they would try and go through it.

When two of the bearded guys came back, they simply opened the door and signaled at Dan. Their rifles were drawn. Dan followed one of them, while the other stayed behind him. In that formation, they walked down the narrow corridor. Wind blew against the sides of the wall. A panel of flat rectangular windows opened high above his head, more than three meters high. That wind must be coming from the ocean, he thought.

They passed a series of doors until they came to one and knocked. A voice told them to enter. Dan walked in and blinked in surprise. An older man with silvery hair was sat at the table. McBride.

McBride indicated to the two men. They left the room and shut the door. McBride stood up. His skin was leathery from the sun, and his slate grey eyes quick and sharp.

Dan said, "Fancy seeing you here."

"Do you know why I'm here?" McBride countered.

Dan was thinking. After a few seconds pause, he said, "You bought me the ticket for that plane to Atlanta. Guess I fell for it."

"What do you mean?"

"You knew that Jody Longworth would be on that flight."

McBride said, "Yes, I did."

Dan asked, "What else?"

"Nothing else, Dan. I knew Philip was missing. I had a feeling something might happen, but I did not know for sure."

"You knew they were after her."

"Yes, I did."

Dan sighed. "Can we stop playing games here? Pretty sure you have been listening to my cell phone, so you must know where Jody and Tanya are. Just tell me the rest already."

"What do you think is going on?" McBride asked.

"Philip Longworth knew something important. It's not about broadband cables. That's a cover. The two folders I picked up from Marcus Schopp's desk were classified information from the Navy. They were about clandestine undersea platforms. Designed for unmanned undersea vehicles. Philip must have known something critical about them."

"What else?"

"Synchrony Communications has to be a front company for the DoD.

They work closely with DARPA, and Marcus used to work for DARPA."

McBride said, "That's right. Marcus Schopp was the head of the Tactical Technology Office. He got to know Philip while DARPA was funding the work of another company called Dynamic Corp."

"Yes, that was the company that went bankrupt."

"Correct. They became close friends. Philip had money worries and Marcus got him to work for him."

"What did Philip do exactly?"

McBride paused and went back to his chair. He put some folders inside a drawer and locked it. "Follow me, son."

CHAPTER 33

Dan hurried down the corridor behind McBride. They walked out into a clearing. The ocean lay behind them. They crossed the clearing into a huge warehouse. The guards at the front saluted and let them in.

The place was so vast that Dan couldn't see the end. Its width was easily more than a hundred meters, he guessed. Dozens of workshops lined the floor space. Precision engineering machines hummed over large yellow objects that looked like overturned boats. Dan watched a machine wheel up, driven by a man controlling robotic arms. He used the arms to fix something on the overturned boat closest to them, then went down the line, fixing all of them. McBride pointed to them.

"Undersea pods," he said, as if that explained everything.

"What does that mean?" Dan asked.

"These pods are meant to lie on the sea bed, and I mean deep sea bed, more than two miles down. They hold drones inside them. They can lie there for years, if need be. If they get disturbed, or get a signal, then the pods hatch."

"Hatch?"

"Yes, Dan. They hatch and rise to the surface. Like bubbles. At the surface of the ocean, the pod snaps open and the drone pops out. It lifts into the air and does its survey, sending data in real time. On identifying a target, the drones will carry missiles that can be activated."

Dan digested this in silence.

"So, they're like ISR tools?" ISR stood for intelligence, survey and reconnaissance.

"Yes, precisely," McBride said. "We can't monitor all the oceans. Our nuclear subs are out on deterrent missions all the time. But that's a defensive arrangement and not an adequate one. We need to be more proactive. The new class of nuclear submarines the Russians and Chinese have are so silent, even our extensive sonar receivers aren't picking them up in time."

Dan had been on the nuclear submarine SSGN *Georgia* once as they had been evacuated from *Bandar Khalifa*, a port in Iraq. He remembered how the entire sea seemed to rise up around the RIB to which they clung for life. It had been night time, and he couldn't see a great deal, but the experience of boarding and then being on the nuclear submarine had been etched on his mind. He had great respect for submariners. Those men and women spent months under the oceans, ex-communicated from the rest of the world. They were an exclusive set.

"We don't want to be notified of a Chinese nuclear sub lurking one hundred miles out of Norfolk," Dan said aloud.

"Damn right, son. That's where these pods come in. They have pressure transducers that can be activated by the water displacement of a nuclear sub. They can be powered by ocean currents."

McBride looked at Dan. "Tell me what the problem is here."

Dan thought for a while, then shrugged. "Communication?"

McBride smiled for once. "Good. Salt water doesn't allow radio waves. Hence, we don't have Wi-Fi and GPS under water. It is very hard to communicate from land to deployed submarines. So, these pods become critical. Once activated, we can get all sorts of information from the airborne drones about what's lurking under the sea."

"What else do you think the pods can do?" McBride asked.

"I don't know."

"Well, they can carry unmanned undersea vehicles. Whole swarms of them. When activated, these undersea drones can carry out a variety of missions."

Dan whistled. "So, we don't need submarines anymore?"

"No, we do. But in far fewer numbers."

"I'm guessing these pods and drones will be one hell of a lot cheaper than traditional nuclear subs."

"Think billions of dollars."

"Eyes on the ocean floor," Dan said. "Is this what those folders on Marcus' desk were all about?"

"To a certain extent, yes. But there's more."

Dan asked, "So now we have all these UUV's or drones under water, searching for enemy subs and other threats. How far can they travel?"

"Depends on their fuel, but two to three hundred miles is not impossible."

Dan said, "I think these drones are battery charged, aren't they?"

Mc Bride clicked his fingers. His face became animated. "And batteries run out quickly. Even the most powerful iridium batteries on a UUV won't last for more than a week."

Dan was beginning to see. "I get it. You want to keep these pods as docking stations. They can have electric chargers that can recharge the drone batteries."

"Bingo! So imagine a network of unmanned undersea pods where roving UUV's could stop to recharge their batteries. At the same time, they could securely upload the intelligence they've been collecting, which could be transmitted to a nearby command post on a ship."

"I get it. So, that's why you mentioned the communications. A submarine can't communicate with land easily, not without the risk of being detected. But if the pods are detected, the worse that can happen is that they get destroyed.

"Exactly."

"And the pods will hold drones as well?"

"Yes. They'll have multiple functions. They are forward-deployed battle stations really. UUV's can dock, recharge, upload and be on their way again. If a threat is perceived, the pods can release a float to the surface, which releases the drone."

Dan shook his head. He had not understood much of this from reading the folders, but hearing it from McBride made it sound real. It was mind blowing. A whole network of undersea drones guarding America's coastline from threats.

"I still don't get what you needed Philip for. He is a cable engineer, right?"

McBride lifted a finger. "More than that. He was a specialist in deep sea fiber optic cabling. Ninety-five percent of our internet data comes from these deep-sea cables. Without them, we are powerless. Think of a world without Google, email. That's what would happen if someone severed the cables."

"So, these drones could guard the cables?"

"It's time we went outside," McBride said.

CHAPTER 34

They walked past the clearing towards another giant warehouse. Beyond that, Dan could see the ocean, dark now in the late afternoon light, white top waves fighting over each other restlessly.

They emerged on a pitched road. Four trucks were parked on the side. Where the road ended, there was a long harbor. Dan recognized the ship moored at the harbor. It was the white ship with the open stern he had seen while driving around Barnham. It looked bigger close up. The giant crane loomed over the open back, like a colossal sewing spool. A massive circle of cable was attached to it.

Guards let them enter and McBride walked briskly up the gangplank. Dan craned his neck up at the crane. It was a monster and the huge spool of cable it held in its maw swayed ominously in the breeze.

On the deck, Dan stared at a huge machine in front of him. It was made of yellow painted steel and looked like a tank. It had a plow on one end.

"That is our sea bed plow, Dan." McBride slapped the side of the machine. "This big boy weights thirty-two tons, it's ten meters long and five meters high."

Dan said, "It digs holes for the pods to be placed in."

"Yes. But not cover them, just to lay them in open tunnels." McBride pointed out to sea. "This undersea network is the future of anti-submarine warfare, Dan. Most nukes the Chinese and Russians have are hidden in their submarines. With this network, we can find out where these enemy submarines are. You can imagine how much they would like to get their hands on the whereabouts of this network."

"And Philip was in charge of designing which part of the network?"

"Not all of it, obviously. Mainly the locations of where the pods would be. See, the pods are charged by the ocean currents. Movement is converted into electrical energy. That in turn charges the drones. So, we need to place the pods in places where ocean currents are strong. But that is the critical part. If the location of this distributed network falls into enemy hands…"

"They can destroy them with torpedoes. All this effort is in vain."

McBride turned to him. "Do you understand now why Philip is so important?"

"So, he has all this data?"

"Philip and Marcus were the only two with access to the data. All the files were destroyed, and Philip was the only one with the hard drive. He helped in designing the pods as well. He has extensive experience of working in these conditions. Many people are involved in this, but Philip came up with a location map for the first wave of these undersea pods. Then he vanished with the data."

Dan looked at McBride steadily. "Philip wasn't just a cable engineer."

"Correct."

Dan's mind was working hard. "If the Russian mafia and the Mexican gangs were not threatening Philip and his family, I would say Philip was the bad guy. He was a mole, the spy who was also the scientist."

"Good thinking."

"I want to know how the Russians got to know that Philip had this data. But once they knew, they came after him. They threatened his family. Philip disappeared with the data. Then they killed Marcus."

"Right on."

"Who was Philip really working for?"

McBride said, "FBI."

"Really?"

"Yes, really. Many military technology secrets were ending up in the hands of Russians. We suspected a mole within the Pentagon, or inside some defense contractors. This isn't that rare actually. Defense contractors are technical companies and they often employ talent from abroad. Some foreign scientists have turned out to be spies in the past."

"Hang on. I don't get it. How can Philip be a cable network engineer and an FBI agent?"

"He wasn't an FBI agent. He was helping them. And he was working undercover."

"So, he spread word that he had this secret information, and the Russian gangsters came for him?"

"Something like that."

Dan frowned. "What about the cocaine?"

McBride shrugged. "The Mexicans acted as the enforcers for the Russians. When Philip realized, he played a dangerous double game. He tried to become a dealer for the Mexicans. To see if he could find out who sent them. The plan backfired."

Dan thought for a while then said, "You know he was sick, don't you?"

"Yes. That was sad."

"The pressure of having to work undercover isn't easy either. There was too much on his shoulders."

"Yeah." McBride stared at the horizon, where light was fading in banks of grey and red clouds. "I don't know how this is going to end, Dan. But we need to find Philip and the data. Fast. Before the enemy get to him."

Dan said quietly, "I know where he is."

McBride spun around. "Are you serious?"

"I think I know, sir. We have to go and see." Dan told him about Cumberland Island. McBride listened with a grim face.

"What do you need to do?" he asked when Dan had finished.

Dan laid out his plan, something he had been working on since he left the town hall and police station. McBride listened without interrupting. "Okay. Let me send a crew with you."

Dan shook his head. "No, he's spooked already. If we turn up with the cavalry, he might run again. He needs to trust someone."

Dan levelled a gaze at McBride. "What I want now is you to be honest with me. You dragged me into this. Is there anything else I need to know?"

McBride shook his head. "You know everything I know. People much higher up than me are on this Dan. Make no mistake, this is the highest national security issue at the moment."

A phone rang somewhere. Dan looked towards McBride, who frowned and patted his uniform jacket. He produced a cell phone, checked the number, and answered. Dan watched his face change. He listened, then turned away from Dan. He spoke briefly, then hung up.

"Things just got a whole lot worse," McBride said. His weather-beaten face was pinched, and his voice was edgy.

"A Russian research ship has been seen in the Atlantic, a few meters from where we have important data cables. An Ohio class nuclear sub is on its way. That ship being there can't be a coincidence, Dan. This could be a shit storm in the making. You better find Philip, and find him fast."

CHAPTER 35

Dan got his cell phone back from the guys who arrested him. They were Delta operatives.

The ginger-haired leader said, "I'm sorry we had to do that. But we didn't know who the hell you were."

Dan shook hands with him. "No problem. You did your job. Name's Dan, by the way."

"Fisher. I know your name."

Dan made two phone calls, then called Lisa. She picked up at the first ring.

"Dan, where the hell have you been? Your phone's been silent, like, forever."

Dan explained to her about the car chase.

"Jeez, are you ok?"

"Yes, I'm coming over to get some stuff. Talk to you then." He hung up. He went to the next room, where McBride was debriefing the four Delta guys. They all turned as Dan came in.

Dan walked over to the table where they had opened up a map. Cumberland Island, seventeen miles long and three miles wide, was a ferry ride away from the town of St Mary's and not far from the King's Bay Naval Base. McBride circled the island with a pen. It had a long shape, thin at the bottom and broad at the top. It bent around the contours of the coastline and offered protection to the naval base.

"Where do you think he might be?" McBride asked.

"I don't know," Dan said. "But the island is a national park and gets visitors. I reckon he will head for the northern end, which is more remote. Can we have an RIB in these waters that I can call on?"

"That's easy," Mc Bride said. "You can have two."

"What else?"

155

"I want an infra-red painter, but I can use one attached to a rifle. I will need extra ammo, too. A GPS tracker would be good."

McBride said, "You need a GPS signal for sure. There's going to be a drone above."

"Really?"

"This is important, Dan. We need to get it right the first time. To do that, I want eyes on you."

Dan nodded. It made sense. But he needed to clarify something. "The drone won't have a payload, will it?"

McBride fixed his steely eyes on Dan. "Not if you don't want it to."

Dan shook his head. "Too dangerous. Could be a blue on blue."

"Alright. I've got something for you." McBride leaned across the desk and opened a drawer. He took out a long, curved knife in its scabbard. The handle was thick, with a black rubber grip. It was long, fifteen and half inches, and was more of a machete than a knife.

Dan exclaimed, "A kukri!" McBride handed it to him. Dan took the knife and removed the scabbard. The blade was made of black steel.

"That's a KA Bar kukri made in USA. Thought you might like one."

Dan gripped the weapon and looked at it reverently.

"Thank you, sir. I owe you one." He smiled gratefully at McBride. He strapped the kukri on his back belt. The familiar presence was reassuring.

"You need a car, right?" McBride asked.

Fisher spoke. "There's one waiting for you outside, by the trucks."

Dan said, "I need a gun."

"Follow me," Fisher said. They went down the corridor to the men's quarters. The armory was a walk-in cabinet, locked by a steel wheel safe. Dan looked at the weapons rack and whistled.

"You got anti-tank weapons in here?"

Fisher said, "Prepared for every situation, man."

Dan chose a suppressed Hecker and Koch 417, with the medium range, sixteen-inch barrel. He took a detachable thirty round magazine, each round a full-powered 7.62x51mm NATO ordnance. He took five extra ammo boxes. He chose a Sig Tac CP-4x optical sight for the rifle, and a pair of NVG's for himself.

"Nice choice," said Fisher.

"Gas checked?" Dan asked, indicating the rifle.

"Yup. Ready for battle."

The car outside was a civilian Cherokee jeep. Dan had the rifle and ammo in a shoulder bag. He had taken some extra ammo for the Sig as well. He had the Glock from the gangster he had killed. Along with his kukri, he felt he finally had a decent arsenal.

He shook hands with Fisher and the other Delta guys, then faced McBride.

"Good luck, Dan" the older man said.

Dan said, "For the last time. Right?"

"Right."

Dan got in the Cherokee and drove back to the motel. He left the guns in the trunk and went upstairs. Lisa opened the door before he knocked.

"I heard you coming," she said. Sunlight fell on her face, making her green eyes dance. She wore a white sleeveless vest and shorts. She touched his arm. "You okay?"

"Need to get changed," Dan said as he walked in. "I must stink like a road kill."

Lisa smiled. "After what just happened, I think we can forgive you for that."

Dan took his shirt off and threw it in the bathroom. He noticed Lisa staring at his chest.

"You need to get packed. We might be camping for the night."

"Where are we going?"

"Cumberland Island." Dan told her what happened as he wrapped a towel around himself. "Pack your full sleeves and trunks. Take a hat. You might need to get some bug spray as well. It's a wild island."

He had a quick shower while Lisa got ready. He changed into the dark clothes he had in his backpack, then they both headed downstairs.

CHAPTER 36

They were too late to catch the ferry, but Dan chartered a private boat to taken them across from the mainland visitor's center at St Mary's.

He checked his new GPS watch that the Delta guys had given him. 1800 hours. The sky was still bright, but the sun was a pale shadow over the horizon, shimmering its last light on the sea. Lisa and Dan clambered onto the twenty-foot motorboat. Lisa sat close to Dan and shivered. The captain fired the engines and the boat shook, then chugged forward into the water. They could see the island, a dim, blue shape at the mouth of St Mary's river. As they advanced, a black shape crossed ahead of them. It was very long and a turret rose high above the water, dwarfing the boat.

"That's a submarine," Dan pointed.

"Gosh, it's big."

"Hmm. Pretty special inside, too." Dan told her of the time he had been on the SSGN *Georgia*.

They got off at the Sea Camp dock on the island and waved the boatman goodbye. Dan looked around him.

"We can stay at the Sea Camp tonight, if you want. We'll be hiking tomorrow anyway, so best to get a night's sleep."

"Sure thing," Lisa said.

As they walked off the dock, Dan saw another private boat arrive. They had moved about five hundred yards, but he looked back before they left the dock. A number of men were lifting bags out of the boat. He counted the men. Six in total. He had no problem in recognizing the tall blond man who was helped up by one of the men. Dan ducked into the path at the end of the dock, joining Lisa and dropping out of sight. He grabbed her hand.

"We gotta go," he said.

"What's going on?" Lisa asked, matching her steps to his.

"They're here. The men who tried to kill me." Lisa didn't say anything.

She squeezed Dan's hand and hurried alongside him. They checked into a double bedroom at the Sea Camp. Once they were inside, Dan took out his Sig and went near the window. The lights were off. He could see the main entrance of the camp. He waited, but didn't see any of the men coming in. A light sprang up behind him. It was Lisa coming out of the bathroom. Dan closed the curtains.

"Lisa," he said, "this is going to get nasty. I want you to get out of here now."

"I've come all this way. I want to see this to the end."

Dan shook his head. "No, you don't understand these people. They will kill both of us given half a chance. Tomorrow morning, I want you to take the ferry back to the mainland."

"And what will you do?"

"Start hiking. I need to find Philip. And they'll come after me."

"Give me a gun. I grew up on a farm. I know how to fire one."

"These wild animals shoot back. It's not the same."

Lisa stepped into his face. She was inches away and he could feel the heat of her body. She put a hand on his chest. Dan swallowed. She looked up at him, her emerald eyes full of a mild question.

"We do this together," she whispered. "Do you understand? Two pairs of eyes are better than one. And trust me, I know how to handle myself."

Dan closed his eyes. "Okay, but you stick by me and do exactly as I tell you. Right?"

Lisa nodded slowly. "Like I said, I know how to use a gun. I've done range fighting contests before. If you have a spare one, I could use it."

Dan nodded. "Okay, you could use the Glock. I'll show you tomorrow." He smiled at her. "Now go to sleep."

"How about you?"

Dan pointed to the packed sandwiches they had taken out of Lisa's bag. "I need to eat something, then I'm keeping guard."

"Okay partner. Wake me up at 3:00 a.m., and I'll take over."

Dan sat down on the floor as Lisa got ready for bed. He kept his eyes averted, but didn't miss the stolen looks that Lisa darted in his direction. He munched on the turkey, mustard and gherkin sandwiches they had picked up from the shopping mart on the way.

Night fell.

He could hear waves crashing on the beach outside. Insects buzzed by the lights nearby. He listened hard, waiting for footsteps. The Sig was between his legs. The kukri was strapped to his left thigh. The Glock was on his back belt. He was ready.

He wondered what it was like outside. On the beach, with the waves rushing in, the stars out over the sea like a moth-eaten blanket. Where was Philip? Somewhere near. He would find out tomorrow.

He rubbed his eyes and yawned. That sandwich had made him full. His cell was off and separated from his battery. He went and sat near the window and parted the curtains gently. Yellow light showed the log planks on the pathway outside. Two cabins on either side of him, and the entrance at the front. It was deserted.

He almost dozed off a couple of times, but every time he felt like it, he got up and paced around. He wished he had some coffee. After what seemed like a long time, he felt a movement behind him and he turned around with a start. The Sig was instantly in his hand.

"Whoa!" he heard a female voice cry. Lisa. There was muffled sound. His watch had a light and Dan turned it on. It was bright as a flashlight. Lisa had fallen back on the bed.

"I'm sorry," Dan said, giving her a hand. She caught it and stood up.

"Are you alright?" Dan asked. "Sorry, you startled me."

Lisa went to turn on the bedside light. Dan stopped her.

"I don't want anyone to see inside," he said. Lisa nodded.

"It's my turn for watch," she said.

"Are you sure?" Dan asked.

Lisa said, "Yes, catch some sleep."

Dan needed that. He had a long day tomorrow. He put the weapons under his pillow and tried to sleep.

*****

Morning came bright and boisterous. Dan woke up to find the room bright from sunlight filtering in through gaps in the curtains. Lisa was asleep on the twin bed next to his. 0600 hours. He swung his legs off the bed. The door was shut as it had been all night. He checked it carefully. By the time he had brushed and come out of the bathroom Lisa was up and stretching.

"No sight of the tango's?" he asked.

Lisa was momentarily confused, then her face cleared. "You mean the bad guys. Nope. Guess they need to sleep too."

"Yes, but they won't be far. We need to be switched on today."

Dan packed food, bottles of water, his flashlight, a length of nylon rope and his tatty leather gloves into the backpack. The palm leather gloves were old and had seen use all over the world. The last time had been in Afghanistan, abseiling down from an MH-6 helicopter into a Taliban commander's compound. The mission had been one of his last, and a success. After the end of his combat days, Dan had kept his leather gloves. It was his little piece of luck. He had his old army issue kukri too, but getting on a civilian plane with that was impossible these days.

Lisa came out, wearing her hiking gear. They walked to the Sea Camp offices first, where there was a camping shop. Dan bought a two-man tent, in case they spent the night out in the open. There was every possibility. He got a map and pored over it with Lisa.

"We are here," Dan pointed at the southern tip of the island. "We got a long hike up. These are the hiking trails."

"Look, there's a road that goes up north. Stops halfway up the island. Maybe we can hire bikes," Lisa suggested.

"Good idea," Dan said. They went to the bike hire, Dan keeping his eyes peeled. He reckoned the men would have split up, and dressed like the other holiday makers. It was easy to spot a clump of six men in a camp of families and couples.

He paid for the bikes, then they set off. The sun was climbing and the morning rays were refreshing. They could see the ocean's blue glint up ahead. They passed a crumbling ruin. It had once been a vast building, but only columns of bricks and bare walls remained. Dan looked behind him as he cycled. He cycled slower, deliberately, to let Lisa go ahead, and also to keep watch behind him. In the distance he could see a number of cyclists. It was impossible to be sure if they were being followed.

They took a break at 9:00 a.m., and then cycled again. An hour later they had come to the end of the road. A hiking trail went inside the island, and the same road curved into a branch that led to the white sand dunes by the sea.

Lisa was off her bike and down on the hiking trail. "Jeez, I am pooped."

Dan nodded. "We rest here." He handed her a water bottle. He got off his bike and looked behind him. A couple of bikers went past. Looked like a family. Others were coming up behind. All seemed to be following the road.

He looked at his watch. "Our path is straight up from here, if we want to go to the northern tip of the island."

Lisa took a gulp of water and wiped her mouth. "Let's go."

They walked up a few paces on the trail, then Dan took their bikes and put them behind an oak tree. He chopped some bush with his kukri and scattered the leaves and twigs over the bikes, concealing them.

CHAPTER 37

The ocean on either side had turned grey against grey clouds that had claimed the sky. Dan didn't mind. If they had to hike, a blistering noonday sun was the last thing he needed. Especially with Lisa with him. It wasn't like he could leave her to rest. The Russians weren't far behind.

The trail led deeper into the trees covered with Spanish moss, and soon they had lost sight of the ocean. Branches and twigs leaned over the path. The oak trees were twisted, and palmetto fronds crowded around their roots. The gnarled branches and the light filtering in through the leaves made the place look strange, mythical.

Dan took out his kukri and hacked at the branches, making it easier for Lisa to walk.

"Looks like you done this before," Lisa panted.

"Many times. I did operations in Borneo, south Asia. Basically, I was let loose in a tropical forest in the middle of monsoon, to track down the leader of an insurgent group. That darned place was full of leeches, snakes and swamps. Once you live through that, the rest becomes easy."

"Glad you feel that way."

Dan stopped and glanced back. "Are you okay?"

Before Lisa answered, there was a scurrying noise in the bushes below. A long, oval-shaped creature emerged near their feet, its long snout pointing at their feet. Lisa screamed and jumped on Dan. Dan caught her easily and lifted her up.

"Don't worry," he said. "That's just an armadillo."

"Jesus Christ, that scared me," Lisa looked embarrassed. She got off from Dan, brushing her legs. "Sorry."

"Don't be." He pointed a few feet away. It was a pile of horse manure.

"That's horse dung, but I think they have other animals, too. I can tell by the paw marks." Dan showed her. "That's either deer or hogs."

Lisa crinkled her nose. "Smells," she said.

A flight of birds got Dan's attention. It came from a clump of oak trees that they had left behind. About a hundred meters away. He clamped his jaws tight. He took out his Glock and showed Lisa how to use it.

"You walk ahead now," he said. "We might have company. Keep looking all around you, not just ahead. But be careful of your arc of fire." He made a semi-circle with his hands and Lisa nodded.

They walked quicker with Dan glancing back frequently. The forest around them was dense. Some animal trails branched off from the path, but none wide enough for humans. Dan had the kukri back in its scabbard. The Heckler and Koch was in his arms now, trigger finger where it should be. He moved in circles as he followed Lisa, pointing the rifle in 360 degree arcs.

Sounds came from around them. A quick rustle of steps to his left stopped Dan in his tracks. The gangsters would move into the bush, he knew that. They would try and attack them from the sides. Behind him, Lisa had heard it as well. Her Glock arm was extended.

"Keep moving," he hissed. "Stay low."

The rustle came again and Dan raised his weapon, head up from the optical sight, ready to fire at will. A horse broke out from the shrub. Dan sighed and lowered his weapon. He scanned around him. Nothing. He stepped back, facing the other way to Lisa.

"Move," he said.

They kept walking, eyes and ears tuned to every sound in the forest. The trees above them started to get thinner. The ground had been flat, but it started to climb a trail. They pushed on. Several times, they heard sounds, and they squatted down, guns ready. But apart from animals, they saw nothing. Dan was uneasy. He knew they were being followed. They had probably found the bikes. Just how far down they were, he didn't know. After last time, they were keeping their distance and biding their time.

The path trailed down again and Dan heard the faint sound of galloping hooves and neighs. He looked down. Lisa had stopped.

The ocean was closer to their left and the hill sloped down to meet the white dunes on the beach. Scattered at the bottom of the hill were large felled oak trees, their branches sticking up like accusing fingers. The beach was very wide, perhaps the widest expanse of free beach Dan had seen. The clouds were less and the light had changed, making the ocean appear more blue. White crested waves charged to the beach and Dan's eyes followed the pack of wild horses that ran across, splashing water and neighing loudly. It was remote and forsaken, nature at its primordial, inchoate, best. At any other time, he would have sat down to enjoy the spectacular view.

Then he saw the huts.

In the shade of the hill's slope, to the extreme right. They caught his eye as he followed the horses. Three dilapidated log cabins, Spanish moss heavy on the walls, sitting on wooden platforms. Although old and not maintained, they were sturdy and had withstood the vagaries of nature. Dan signaled to Lisa. They left the trail and waded into the bush. Dan went first. He took the Sig in his right hand and held the kukri in the left. He slashed hard at the bush around him, taking care at his feet.

"Look out for snakes," he said to Lisa. "Don't jump over if you see one. Give it a wide berth and walk around."

"Rattlesnakes?"

"Yup."

Lisa's face said it all. Dan looked behind him. If the Russians were following, they were doing a damn good job of hiding. They arrived at the base of the hill unhurt. Dan was the first to jump on the powdery white beach. He helped Lisa down.

They crouched and observed. The three huts were about fifty meters away. He indicated, and Lisa moved first. Dan looked up and back as soon as Lisa was mobile. He crept forward with his back to her. The rifle was back in his hands, pointing up at the forest above and behind him. The huge expanse of the beach was totally empty. The ocean lay in the distance with the rolling sound of the breakers. He looked behind—Lisa was close to the first cabin. He ran, his feet digging into the powdery white sand.

Together, they stared at it. It looked much worse close up. Moss grew all over it. Moisture had rotted most of the timber and a section of the roof had fallen in. The two windows that faced the ocean were shut. Wooden shutters.

The door too was closed. Dan indicated, and Lisa sank to her knees, gun arm extended. Dan crept forward. The smell of animal waste was strong. The platform creaked under his feet. He got up to the door. It was locked. He took a step back and kicked it hard. There was a splintering sound, and the door crashed inwards. Dan had leaped to one side already, back pressed to the logs. He looked at Lisa, who nodded.

Dan peered in. It was hard to see in the gloom inside. He took his flashlight out. It was empty inside. Old wood, overgrown with moss, and a stench that came from being shut for decades came from within. Dan stepped in and flashed the light around. No one had been in this room apart from the wind and some critters.

Lisa was out already and rushing to the next cabin. Dan followed. Lisa seemed to be a quick learner. She sank to her knees outside the cabin, gun raised. Dan ran past her and kicked the door down. The door crashed open. The smell of waste was less this time. On Lisa's signal, he went in. This cabin was better preserved. It was sandwiched between the two and its side walls were in good shape. There was a hole in the roof, through which light penetrated, and a damp spot had formed in the middle from rain.

In one corner, Dan found what he expected. A camping bed on the floor. Two bottles of water to one side of it, and a laptop.

He flashed his light over it. He knelt down. Under the pillow, he found a cell phone that was turned off. He picked up the laptop. It had a remote battery charger connected to it. He heard a sound behind him and saw Lisa come in.

Lisa had both hands on the Glock, pointing straight at Dan.

"Put your hands in the air, Dan," Lisa said.

CHAPTER 38

Dan stopped. He put the cell and the laptop under the pillow. He stayed kneeling on the floor.

"I said, put your hands in the air, damn it." Lisa's voice was harsh.

Dan slowly put his hands up.

"Turn around. Easy." Lisa said.

Dan did as he was told. He stood up, and the room suddenly seemed small with both of them in it. Lisa was standing with her feet apart, in line with her shoulders. The Glock was pointed straight at Dan's head. At this close range, he knew she wouldn't miss.

"Take off your backpack and the rifle. Very slowly."

Dan did as he was told, not taking his eyes off Lisa.

"Now the Sig. Kick them all to me. Any funny moves and I fire."

Dan took his Sig out and put it on the floor, next to the rifle and backpack. He nudged them towards her with his foot.

"Now kneel back down, and put your hands behind your head."

Dan knelt. "You're the double agent, aren't your Lisa?" he asked. Lisa didn't reply.

Dan said, "It was you who introduced Philip to the Russian gangster. When Philip realized who the gangster was, he made a run for it. Yes, he was sick. He needed money. For medical bills and college fees. You preyed on him and got him to meet the Russians."

Lisa remained motionless, her gun not wavering.

"Only, you got it wrong, Lisa. You underestimated Philip. He agreed to meet with your man, because he wanted to flush them out. That was why he had an escape plotted out."

"Shut up," Lisa said, frowning.

"You spies are all the same. You think you're so goddamn clever. But you're actually stupid. The Mexicans followed me back from Tanya's college after I told you I was going there. That was a giveaway. Marcus was shot dead that morning I was in your apartment. You left early, way early. I saw you slip out of the apartment. He was shot dead in his car that morning. That was why you knew about it before anyone else. Andy Brown told me on the phone and no one else knew. No one at Synchrony. No one in the media. How the hell did you know? That was pretty dumb of you."

Lisa's face had lost some of its composure. She came forward, her jaws working. "You don't know what the hell you're talking about, Dan. Save your breath, 'cos you're going to die soon."

Dan smirked. "Those DoD reports you showed me about Marcus? The ones from the Pentagon? They were fakes. Good ones, but fakes. I took photos of them on my cell phone. I sent them to my friends. You were trying to convince me Marcus was the bad guy, when Marcus was actually the only friend Philip had. I bet you he was the one who helped Philip escape. He might also have been the only one who knew where Philip was. That was why you had to kill him."

"You son of a bitch. Should have killed you too, when I had the chance."

"Yes, you should have. Because, you know what? You're not going to get that data. Ever. You'd better tell that research ship out there to turn back unless it wants to get blown sky-high."

Lisa bared her teeth. "Wrong, dickhead. All the data is in that laptop right there. I just need to take it." She paused. "By the way, if you're so darned smart, then why did you let me come all the way with you here?"

"To get the Russians out of Barnham. I didn't want them lurking around the base. I knew they would follow us. And, I wanted *you* right where I could keep an eye on you."

Dan smiled again, and Lisa didn't like it. Her eyes snaked to the bed, then back to Dan.

"You want the laptop, you have to get through me first," said Dan, and stood up. Lisa fired. The hollow clicks of the pin on the chamber sounded twice.

Lisa looked like she had been punched in the gut. She fired again and the hollow click sounded again.

Dan put his hand inside his pockets and took out the rounds.

"I took them out last night. That's why I waited until today to give you the gun." He threw the rounds on the floor. They clattered around Lisa's feet.

Lisa snarled and jumped on Dan. She punched him. He ducked and the blow glanced off his shoulder. He straightened and caught her on the chin with an upper cut. Lisa went flying across the room and crashed against the wall. She slid to the floor, dazed. Dan knelt by the backpack. He removed the nylon rope and tied her hands together, then used the same length of rope to tie her hands to her legs. He ripped off a piece of the bedding with his kukri and stuffed her mouth with it. She could still breathe through her nose.

It was an acutely sharpened auditory sense that made him duck the split second he heard the sound.

A battle-hardened sixth sense wired inside him for life. It saved him, as it had done in the past.

The heavy round smashed in through the window on the side, and thudded into the woodwork where a second before, his head had been.

Bop. Bop. Bop.

He recognized the sound of suppressed rounds—they burst in from the window. Dan looked towards the door. He could hide from the window, but the door was the danger zone. If they came in through there, he was good as dead. That would be their plan: pin him down with fire, and send a killer to the door.

He looked for the guns. They were by his feet. The bullets kept coming in from the window, whining and banging inside. He ignored it. He backed up against wall, the Heckler and Koch pointed at the door. The doorframe moved, and then was kicked open. Dan fired from the hip. His first rounds caught the man in the doorway square on the chest, spinning him backwards. The man behind him had no chance either. Dan had shuffled forward on the floor. As the front man fell, Dan was firing already. Two 7.62mm NATO rounds made mincemeat of the second man's face. The third guy was standing with his back to the wall outside. He thought he had his chance now. But he was wrong.

This was close-quarter battle and Dan had never fought it with one weapon. The rifle was too heavy to move quickly. The third guy knew this. He exposed himself, pointing his gun at Dan. But he had not expected Dan to be so close to him.

Too late, he saw the snout of the Sig Sauer pointing at him, a mere five feet away. Shot one blew his face away, and shot two severed the spine below the neck, so the automatic impulse that made him squeeze the trigger, even after he was brain dead, was no longer a factor.

There was no one else outside. The shots coming in from the window had stopped. Dan heard a volley of shots from further out, up in the hill. Sounded like a different weapon. He knew who that was.

Andy Brown. That was one of the phone calls he had made after speaking to McBride. The other had been to Tanya. Dan looked around the beach, then rolled out of the hut. He turned and scrambled to the base of the hill. Holding the rifle aloft with one hand, he hoisted himself up on the slope. He rushed up, rifle at the shoulder now, scanning around. He heard more shots up front. A round whined above his head. He dropped flat, then threw himself against the trunk of an oak tree. He needed to find the source of fire.

More rounds came. He leaned out the side and let out a volley himself. Then he ran for the next tree. He wasn't fast enough, but he got lucky.

A thick branch snapped in two in a burst of fire at hip height, just as he got to the cover of the tree trunk. Shrapnel and dust exploded into his face. That round was headed straight for his liver. He thanked the tree and laid down heavy fire in that direction. His ammo ran out. He clipped another thirty round magazine and began firing. He didn't stop, and the clump of trees he was firing to became pockmarked with dark spots as chunks of the trees blew away. He emptied the magazine, reloaded and laid down rapid fire again.

There was a method to his madness. He had counted six last night at the harbor. Three were dead. If the other three were holed up here, then he could finish the job now.

He had Andy Brown bringing up the rear. If he could distract the gangsters, they wouldn't hear Brown coming up behind them, and Brown could waste them all. With any luck. He spotted a flash of white against the trees in front and fired. There was a scream and he was fired upon immediately.

Dan heard more screams, and the sound of new fire came in. That was Brown. The familiar sound of the M4 assault rifle came again and Dan heard more screams. The gangsters were trapped and had to escape. Dan was ready. One of the gangsters made a run for it. Dan tracked him for two seconds, then got him with a head shot. He saw a blur of movement to his left, but he was too late to aim and fire. Then he heard another burst of M4. The man went down in a heap.

Four and five down. Which left one.

CHAPTER 39

Silence. All of a sudden, there was no sound. The smell of gunfire hung heavy in the air. Dan did a Sit Rep. All clear.

He listened for a while. Apart from the surf breaking below, the forest was quiet. Dan chewed his lower lip. If the last one was there, it could be trouble. There would be no way of smoking him out unless he moved. Dan knew the art of laying in silence for hours. Targets moved sooner or later. More often than not, it was their last move.

The silence was shattered by the M4 again. Dan gripped his rifle. He didn't have any ammo left. He took the Sig out. Then he heard a shout.

"Dan, are you there?" It was Brown. "Dan?" Definitely his voice. But still, he was careful. He relaxed when a girl's voice sounded.

"Dan, it's Tanya." Shouting meant giving his position away. But now he knew it was them. He leaned out and shouted back.

"There's one left. Have you seen him?"

"No," Brown said. "But we got the two dead ones here."

Dan crawled out of his position. He crawled over the brush to the bodies. Three heads popped up in front of him. Tanya looked scared, but her face cleared when she saw him. He felt sorry for her being here, but there was no way Philip would have gone with Brown.

Next to Brown, he saw an old man. Philip Longworth. The man looked like a ghost. The skin on his face was stretched so tight it seemed to shine. His cheeks were hollows, and so were the holes that were his eyes. A few wisps of hair stuck out from the sides of his scalp. With difficulty, Dan identified him to the man he had seen in the photo. Dan nodded at him. Philip nodded slowly back, staring at him.

The time for pleasantries would be later. They still had an unfinished job. Dan got closer to them.

"Where is he?" he asked them. All three of them shrugged.

"There was a tall, blond guy near the edge of the hill," Tanya pointed towards the ocean. They were far into the forest. Dan suddenly thought of the bullets that were fired at the cabin. They couldn't have been fired by someone here. They had to be at the edge. The leader. The tall guy. He had been taking the shots.

In a flash, he realized. "He's down at the cabin. Might have figured out I'm holding Lisa in there. He wants to get the laptop as well."

"Don't worry about the laptop," Philip said in a low voice, and coughed into his hands. "I have the data in a drive." He reached inside his shirt and showed them a necklace with a pendant at the end. The pendant was a removable disk drive.

"Suits you, sir," Dan said. "You guys stay here to keep watch. I'm going down. Andy, you get up to the edge of that hill now. Use your height to fire on him. Got that?" Andy nodded.

Dan got up and ran to the edge of the hill, then scrambled down to the beach. He ran towards the cabins. His rifle was without ammo. He took out his Sig and slowed down. As he approached the middle cabin, through the window he could see movement inside. A face looked up and saw him.

Dan fired, but not before he had been fired upon. He threw himself on the sand. Another shot whined overhead. Dan got up and ran towards the cabin. He was out in the open, while the blonde guy was inside. He needed to get cover.

Dan fired twice at the window to keep the man quiet. He ran towards the door, but the door opened before he could get there. A tall blond man stepped out. He was big, almost six five, and broad. The wooden platform sagged under his weight. He aimed at Dan, but Dan was quicker.

The Sig jerked twice in his hand and the man screamed. Dan had aimed for his gun hand. A splash of red appeared and the gun flew away. Dan fired again, but the Sig was out of ammo. He was out of ammo, period. The blonde guy realized. With an oath, he used his good hand and scrambled for his gun. He had to turn his back to Dan to do so. Dan had seconds to act. He ran up and cannoned into him.

The cabin shook on its foundation as the two men collided. Dan was up first. He kicked the man's Glock pistol into the sand.

Valcheck Ivanov stood up behind Dan. With his good left hand, he took out a long knife from his belt strap. Dan turned around just as Val thrust forward with the blade. The serrated edge flashed in the sun. Dan stepped aside, but the knife ripped along the side of his forearm. Dan winced in pain. A red gash appeared on his shirt and blood dripped into his hand.

Dan pivoted, slammed into Val and the two men rolled off the platform onto the sand. Dan fought to grab Val's knife hand. He got a hand around it, then lifted his other elbow and brought it down with savage force on Val's chin. Val grunted and tried to punch Dan back. Dan lifted himself off Val and ran. Val got up and followed. He thought Dan was searching for the Glock. But he was mistaken.

Dan took out his kukri with a flourish. Blood dripped down his arm, soaking his grip on the knife. Val snarled as he stood up. They circled each other. The ocean roared behind them. Val's right hand was a bloody mess, but his left arm was strong. Dan suspected the man was ambidextrous, hence the knife had been in his left belt. Val was bending down low. He feinted at Dan, who swayed away easily. He feinted again, lower this time. In a blur of movement, his injured hand grabbed sand and flung it into Dan's face.

Dan coughed and stumbled back. He fell and rolled over, a red mist in his eyes.

He could see Val above him, bearing down for the killer blow. Dan kicked his legs as hard as he could. He caught Val at the knees and they folded. Dan was up as Val lost his balance. The sand was still in his eyes, but he could see. Val rushed him, aiming low again, as most knife fighters did. Dan slapped the knife away with his free hand, and slashed at Val's neck. The longer, hooked blade of the kukri smashed into the neck with a tearing force, severing the arteries immediately. Blood spurted up in a high arch as the kukri cut open the windpipe and came out the other side.

Vyalchek Ivanov fell to his knees. His hands clutched his neck, but they couldn't stop the blood gushing out onto the soft, white sand.

He stared uncomprehendingly at Dan for a second, then slowly his eyes glazed. His body tilted forward and he slumped face-down.

Dan stepped back, panting. Sweat was pouring down his face. He wiped his forehead with the kukri hand. Sweat mixed with blood appeared on his sleeve.

"Goodbye, Dan," a female voice said behind him. He was facing the ocean, and he turned around slowly. Lisa had come out from the cabin. Someone had cut through her ropes. It must have been Val. She had Val's Glock in her hands. It was pointed straight at Dan's head, held in both her hands.

"Are you going to shoot me?" Dan asked.

"You bastard. You spoilt everything."

Dan saw her fingers tighten, and he moved to the left and down. Lisa was right-handed. If the bullet hit his arm or his shoulder, he might still survive. The gun exploded. Dan buried his face in the sand, expecting the sudden stab of pain that came with a bullet wound.

From this range, it would be last his last bullet wound.

It didn't come. There was another explosion, this time from closer by. These shots were coming from behind Lisa. Dan looked up. Lisa was on the sand. A red circle was spreading on her back. The second shot had hit higher up, near the shoulder. Dan saw movement. Andy Brown jumped down from the hill and clambered towards him in the sand.

Dan took the Glock away from Lisa. He turned her over. Her eyes were still open. They flickered as she looked at Dan. Dan shook his head. He checked her wounds. One bullet was inside her chest. Heavy internal bleeding. The other had hit the left shoulder and exited. He pressed on the chest wound, stemming the blood flow.

She might be saved, if there was a helicopter to take her away. Dan took out the GPS locator from his pant pocket and pressed a button. He continued to put pressure on Lisa's chest wound. A sound of motors came from the ocean. An RIB, its black nose rising up above the waves, was bobbing over to the beach at high speed. It landed and Dan watched the four Delta guys pull the boat to shore. He turned to Andy Brown.

"Thank you," he said. Andy only had a revolver in his hand.

"He fired," Andy pointed behind him. Dan looked to see Philip stumbling towards them, the M4 assault rifle pointed towards the sand. He seemed to be weighed down by the gun. But hatred sparkled in his eyes.

When he came up to them, he panted, "Is that the bitch who tried to kidnap my girl? I'll kill her!" he shouted, raising the gun. Dan stepped between them.

"Philip," he said, raising his voice, but keeping himself calm. "She's half-dead already. She's going to get her due, don't worry. If she lives, she can answer a lot of questions. It's better to have her alive."

Tanya was watching with a scared expression on her face. Philip looked wildly from Lisa to Dan.

"It's over Philip. I know what she did. But it's over," Dan repeated. "Look at me."

Philip stared at Dan, who grabbed the muzzle of the gun. He pulled it gently. Philip resisted, but then gave it up.

Tanya came up and put her arm around her father. Then she pointed to Dan's arm.

"You're hurt."

Dan was still holding the kukri. He wiped the blade and put it back in its scabbard. He smiled at Tanya. "This? It's nothing. You're safe, that's what matters."

Her face was drawn and lined with worry. She left her father and came over to hug Dan. He closed his eyes. Relief washed over him. If anything had happened to her, he would never have forgiven himself.

"I couldn't have done this without you," Dan said.

Tanya said, "I'm just glad it's over."

He nodded. "Me, too." He glanced over at Philip. He was a shell of the man he once had been. His back was stooped, his cheeks were caved in. He could barely stand up.

"You okay?" he asked. Philip mumbled something incoherent, and flopped down onto the sand.

The medic in the Delta team gave Lisa emergency aid and called a bird to airlift her. Dan and the others took shelter inside the cabin as the Blackhawk bird touched down. It was back up within seconds, heading for the nearest ER. They wanted Lisa alive.

They picked up Philip's stuff and walked back to the RIB with the remaining two Delta guys. They fired the boat up and it ploughed into the ocean, cutting through the waves powerfully. The boat circled around the mouth of St Mary's river and headed for King's Bay Naval Base. Two men in white uniforms were waiting for them. They escorted them inside. Dan shook hands with the Delta guys. As they walked into the base, he fell in step with Philip.

"I am Dan Roy, he said.

Philip nodded. "Yes, I know who you are. Tanya told me." Philip stopped, and raised his yellow eyes to Dan. "Thank you for looking after my family."

"No problem", Dan said.

"Why did you start buying cocaine off the Mexicans?" Dan asked.

"They were following me around. I wanted to find out why. That's why I approached them. It didn't work out."

Dan said, "That's what I figured."

CHAPTER 40

"Captain, what are we going to do?" Sasha looked at Shevchenko.

They were standing on the bridge, staring out the large glass screens. Men lifted machine parts in the front deck below them. They were being moved out of sight. Shevchenko had a pair of binoculars and he was staring at the thumb-sized speck that had appeared on the north-east horizon. The shape was moving. He lowered the binoculars.

"That is a US Navy destroyer. Not just any other ship," he said quietly. "Did you call the Kremlin?"

"Yes, Captain. They want us to respond, if we are engaged."

"Respond?" Shevchenko sighed. The earlier fight had gone out of him. "Respond against a nuclear submarine and a destroyer with torpedoes?"

"But Captain, you said you did not want this ship to fall into enemy hands."

"Yes, I did. But only if they engaged us. I don't think they will. We are more than two hundred miles away, out of the exclusive economic zone the Americans have from their shores. They suspect us of something, but they will not want an international incident by boarding us, or firing."

"So what do we do?"

"We are in international waters. We hold our ground."

The telephone jangled on the wall. Sasha picked it up. He listened, then turned to Shevchenko.

"Captain, they have located our bandwidth. The Americans are contacting us."

Shevchenko swore under his breath. It had to happen sooner or later. They were listening to all their conversations. With any luck, they hadn't broken the encryption code. But one could never be sure. Without speaking a word, he took the receiver from Sasha's hand.

"This is Captain Mikhail Shevchenko of the Russian Deep Water

Research Agency speaking," he said in perfect English.

There was a pause, and some static, then a voice came through the phone. "This is Admiral John Sims of the United States Navy. Do you copy?"

"Yes I do." An Admiral. That was serious. Probably calling from a land link and not actually on the destroyer. Shevchenko had a sick feeling in the pit of his stomach.

"I know who you are, Captain. I need to tell you something important. Your agent is dead. We know everything about your operation." He paused. "You have two options. One, to head back immediately where you came from. We will be tracking you. If you, or any Russian submarines, are not clear from these waters in the next hour, then you will face option two."

Shevchenko said, "Which is what?"

Another pause, then Admiral Sims continued. "We will confiscate your ship and crew. If you try to resist, we will use force. Your actions are harmful to American interests and we have proof of that. I know you are in international waters, but the Unites States Navy has the right to respond to dangerous intent with force, and by any means necessary. Do you understand?"

"What do you think will happen, Admiral, if you confiscate our ship? Do you think the Russian Navy will sit quietly and allow it?"

"We have assets in the ocean now which are capable of using lethal force against any naval units. This is not a negotiation. We have the absolute right to protect ourselves. Take this as a final warning."

Shevchenko was quiet. He felt old suddenly, and weary. Admiral Sims spoke crisply on the phone again.

"One hour, Captain." He hung up.

Shevchenko handed the receiver back to Sasha.

"What happened, Captain?"

Shevchenko didn't speak for several seconds. He stared out at the choppy blue waves, their white tops curling over like never-ending question marks.

"Sometimes, Sasha, discretion is the better part of valor." He turned and clasped his hands behind his back.

"It is time to go home."

CHAPTER 41

Atlanta
Georgia

Philip Longworth and Dan sat with McBride in a parked car in downtown Atlanta. Two black SUV's were positioned in front and behind them. A black suited agent was out of each car, keeping an eye on the otherwise vacant street.

"The Russian diplomat has been summoned to the White House," McBride said. "The guy you killed, Vyalchek Ivanov, has an uncle who is the secretary to the First Minister of the Russian Navy. The Kremlin is, of course, denying all knowledge of any links. But this is not the first time the Russian mafia has worked with Kremlin. The *Bratva* is an efficient and well-connected global network."

He looked at Dan and Philip and said, "I cannot tell you the name of individuals. But know this: the principal resident of the White House sends his personal regards."

Dan remained silent. Men like him never got medals. They died in cold graves in foreign lands. Dan did not care about politicians. He never would. But he had been able to avoid a calamity for his country – that was the only gratification he needed.

"Were the town hall people of Barnham in on this?" Dan asked.

Philip answered before McBride could. "Yes. We had to take them on board. They fed the usual news to the media. But all they knew was that it was a confidential site. They didn't have details."

Dan asked Philip, "So, did you suspect Lisa Chandler from the beginning?"

"She tried to get close to me all the time. She knew I was in charge of the network design and location. I began to leave hints about my financial problems. That's when it became obvious she was crooked."

"Did she know you had the only copy?"

"She figured it out eventually. No one is allowed copies from the secure room."

"Who is she?"

"A deep undercover agent of the former KGB. Been in this country for fifteen years." Philip coughed into his hands, a hack that bent his back.

"Are you alright?" Dan asked. Philip nodded, getting his breath back.

McBride said. "Her real name is Lydia Vasilevina. By the way, she's alive."

Dan nodded. "Philip needs to get back to the medical center."

"All bills will be paid by us, Philip," McBride said. "When we told the FBI your medical bills weren't coming out of their budget, they loved you even more."

Dan said to McBride, "I need to have a word with you."

McBride said, "Let's step outside." Philip remained in the car.

Dan and McBride walked a few steps away from the car. Dan said, "It ends here."

McBride said, "Yes, I know."

"Like hell you do. Don't play games with me, McBride. I'm not one of your agents anymore. Stop acting like I am one. You should have told me the truth from the beginning. Instead, you let me fall into the shit."

McBride was silent. Dan said, "If Jody asked me for help, you knew I would not refuse." Dan breathed out. "The days of you guys taking advantage of me are over. Do you understand?"

McBride smiled ruefully. "And what about you, Dan? Will you be happy? What the hell are you gonna do with your life?"

Dan said harshly, "That's my god damned concern. All I want is you, and the rest of Washington, and the Government to stay the hell out of my business."

McBride nodded. "Roger that."

Dan walked back to the car. The door opened and Philip stepped out. He stuck his hand out at Dan.

Philip said, "Thank you for everything, Dan."

Dan shook hands with Philip. "Take care of yourself, and your family, Philip," he said.

Philip's eyes were misty. "Words cannot express how I feel."

Dan held Philip's thin shoulder. "It's alright. I understand. Say goodbye to Jody and Tanya for me."

"I definitely will. Where are you headed, Dan?"

Dan said, "Where my two eyes take me. I want to vanish for a while. Where no one can find me."

Dan lifted the backpack on his shoulder, the only luggage he ever carried. He walked to the end of the street, and hailed down a cab. Before he got in, he looked back once. McBride was standing there, looking at him. Their eyes met one last time. Then Dan was in the car, telling the driver to head for the airport.

THE END

Also by Mick Bose:

HIDDEN AGENDA (Dan Roy Series 1)
THE TONKIN PROTOCOL (Dan Roy Series 3)
SHANGHAI TANG (Dan Roy Series 4)
SCOPRION RISING (Dan Roy Series 5)
DEEP DECEPTION (Dan Roy Series 6)

STANDALONE THRILLERS

ENEMY WITHIN – A thrilling manhunt set in USA during WW1.
LIE FOR ME – A complex psychological thriller.
DON'T SAY IT – A stunning suspense thriller.

CPSIA information can be obtained
at www.ICGtesting.com
Printed in the USA
LVHW080035120320
649817LV00017B/958

9 781521 715840